WATER

TO

WATER

Memoirs

Of a

Village Child

Franklin Vanderheide

In

Memory

Of

Admiral

Simon

Newcomb

Franklin Vanderheide

Contents:

Preface

We came from the water, each one from a different place. Every location had chosen one man, none of us knowing the other, yet it was the Admiral that had brought us together; the same that would keep us apart. It had quietly seen to these details as we finally became a group in 1979.

My desire to understand did not begin on 9/11, 2001 like so many others; we had been here for a long time. Unlike all other Nationalities; we hardly ever interfered in the course of events if it was connected to our Host Nation. Fate had placed me here; I was alone at the wheel of a very unique destiny. I would not abandon this position nor could I communicate in a secure manner from a small remote Island at the mouth of Portland Harbor. I would have to make a difficult choice in a few days.

I hadn't ended up there randomly, yet I could not think of any concrete reason why I had to be here at all, especially, on an old Military Base. What I could not explain that day would be kept as a secret while my own secrets kept evading my memory. In time, I would grasp what had been haunting me these last few years.

Most of the Government would be documenting the first hijackers had begun their odyssey only a few miles from where I now stood. My presence had been used; my past interpreted as a sacrifice for a greater good which surely did not exist in that time or any other before September 11th, 2001.

I had already been sacrificed years earlier under similar circumstances which either made me very naïve or quite guilty; the latter being most likely in the interests of others. If the Vice President and CIA wanted to get rid of "The Base" and Osama bin Laden, then this was the perfect cue. The realization that I was one step from being included in those events left me no other choice than to withdraw into 'The Thinker Pose.' The famous Rodin Statue would always come to mind and so would Pugwash.

It could have been that a similar experience had provoked me to react in what some considered an irrational behavior, but who could say for sure. No one other than us knew about the scenarios eleven years earlier when the Secretary of Defense had generated other ideas on what needed to be done. Actually, as I pondered deeper into thought; I began to see those same images of the 1989 Panama Invasion. This was not a good thing anymore, yet other events materialized in ways that no one could have imagined, none more surprised than me.

On the morning of September 17th 2001, the local Newspaper printed the story of a Canadian man in a kayak who tossed a waterproof container of poetry on the jetty of the Coast Guard Station. This action limited Portland Harbor to only two Oil Tankers at a time because of

Security Concerns; a few knew why while the rest of us understood; "any more than two?"

"The Rubaiyat" of Omar Khayyam, the Persian Poet took no prisoners as it made its way from Coast Guard Station, South Portland. At the University of New Hampshire, the exodus was just beginning following the invisible line to Boston. There would be repercussions with so many Saudi's living in New England as well as the son of the President of Pakistan in residence just outside of Boston.

I tested my own interpretations of what had happened, but never fully understood the mechanics of it; at least not then. I had not gone to sleep that evening of September 10th, 2001. I tossed, turned and relived what I could not put my finger on or the reasons why. To add injury to insult, I had lost some memory in 1990 which had set me on a course to discover why things had to happen the way they did: I learned about the person someone had put to sleep along the way, but for what reason?

No one had prepared me for that revelation as it unfolded; the knowledge was difficult to come to terms with but the confusion which seemed to be a daily occurrence did subside. I had to re-educate myself on human nature because what I had learned in the early years of my life no longer applied; all things had changed.

Peace and security would soon be coming to an end. Facts would be attached to fiction while fiction would be attached to facts. It would not be easy to write a story that was overshadowed with thoughts of fear, but my survival would depend on it; so would my family's integrity. As the years passed, I understand answering the phone on that fateful day should have been a mistake but in essence; it had saved my life.

I was standing in the garden when the second phone rang.

"Hello." I said.

On the other end of the line, a Lady in distress asked the unthinkable; "did you hear what just happened?"

I already knew, but I had nothing to say as I looked at the Caller-ID; this was to have a subtle meaning somewhere. "Now who was laughing?"

I spoke calmly as I could; "I was expecting it, prepare yourself; there are two." She ignored my statement.

There were gasps and exclamations of how terrible such a thing as this could have happened.

There was only silence on my end until I spoke the unthinkable; "It's all about collateral damage."

I realized my error in making that statement knowing full well that all my communications were being monitored; they had been since 1990. I could have thanked NASA for that; but not yet. In time I would.

The next 60 seconds was filled with dual voices saying; "What do you mean?"

In the next moment, another plane flew into the second building. I could hear the screams on the end of both phone lines.

"Any more than two will disqualify you." This was the motto that the Admiral had installed in each one of us for reasons I was beginning to understand, finally.

"I have to go now," I said with a calm and reassuring voice switching the land line phone off. I laid it down on a wrought iron bench beside me. I shouldn't have been so honest with the woman on the phone, but if I worked for someone, honesty had to be part of that package; I was still holding a cell phone in my left hand.

It was time to place the call. My thoughts were now of another woman as I pressed each button. A whispered voice broke the silence.

"Bonjour" said a woman's voice.

I said; "Are you monitoring what the hell is going on there? Is this it, or do I need to get out of Dodge?"

Overlooking New York Harbor, concealed within a Torch, the eyes and ears of an unknown dimension would enlighten me; it always did. The Torch was the spiritual residence of the VLBA.

The soft voice speaking so eloquently from my cell phone said; "don't leave the Island. I am sending someone to you."

None much of this was making sense, but I trusted her without question. I recollected the previous night's phone conference on the water issues concerning the Base. It was harmless chatter on pipelines but I could not allow myself to neither think the obvious nor imagine the worst; "who could have been listening?"

My thoughts were now on the last time I had been off Island and what had been so different coming back from Downtown Portland. Nothing had changed except for the presence of the Army's only Navy Barge; a technical marvel with no given purpose for the Army to even have a Navy; I had nothing but time on my hands to think of why it was in this place at this moment in time.

There were few choices right now, but far better is it to be in a garden encouraging life rather than taking it. Here I would stay until I could grasp what had happened. I would engage later what the voice had said, but until then, I would place it out of my mind.

I moved the large urn located in the center of the garden to the side removing the granite block which served as its base. I placed the cell phone beneath it. I said a small prayer for the dying and replaced the granite block back into its position. These government phones were completely invisible but that level of privacy would be coming to end very shortly.

I moved the urn back to its rightful position just in front of the wall fountain. The Ram's head was still spewing a small measure of water through its mouth which reassured me that the garden was still the safest place to be in right now. This had not been my call.

The facts will never be truly Americanized or written into public record. True, there were going to be records, but they would have to be buried in places so others could retrieve them when the time was right. Of course, I had not been alone nor the sole occupant of a very unique life; there were others like me.

I had been blessed with a higher power, a good Organization and a not so permanent failed memory. I had lost a good portion of it, but I did have the basics; it was the Admiral's Ear and Counsel; so what if they were not current. Re-education had not been easy.

Unfortunately as the years passed, I had to learn to become someone I could not honestly remember after 1990. I had to introduce myself to the person I had learned to forget. Each time, there would be a silk fabric, the first being mine; then I had to distinguish between a coffin and a parachute. The only thing I knew for sure after the partial memory loss was the funeral of my father, his name, the silky fabric of a coffin, my childhood and the darkness; "yes, the darkness was real." At the bottom of his grave stone was inscribed, "Hiding in Thee."

I had been fairly exposed up to this time, but now I would be considered beyond exposure from my phone conversation. I walked to the side of the building staring at the gates which allowed entry in and out of the Historic District. I understood what would be implied here as time went on.

Dante's gaze into the Gates of Hell from the Play "Divine Comedy" came to mind as I slowly sat down on a small boulder between the Gatehouse and the Buddhists next door. I slipped my hand under my chin all the while leaning forward. Am I to imitate the Thinker or The Poet?

I would ponder my options, some reasons and finally understand why the pose of the statue was a chin on the hand. This was not the "Divine Comedy"; it was "Diamond Cove." This was a long way from Pugwash, Nova Scotia; Home of The Thinkers. It had become just a 'once upon a time.'

If all of this was for my benefit, then there would be more to come finally ending up with me as the #4. The knife was coming, but I did not foresee the Pentagon or Pennsylvania; my supposed end. These last two had not been planned, but had been cast within the shadows of the Moon. They were not mine to monitor.

I was slowly being cast as Lucky Dragon #7 to which the fall-out would more than likely touch anyone who I came into contact with. I understood why she requested that I remain on the Island for now.

Ignorance had been an unacceptable behavior growing up in such a place as Pugwash. The thought processes of believing the truth would keep us free was sadly mistaken in a world system that operated in total secrecy. We were hardly any different, but ours was for good. That had to count for something.

1

It Takes a Village

I grew up in Pugwash; a Village situated on the Northumberland Strait in Nova Scotia. It was known as the "Home of the Thinkers" for its debut as the host of the Pugwash Peace Conferences in 1957; that information being well placed on welcome signs along the roads leading into this tiny Canadian village. The notoriety became its sense of pride.

Pugwash had not been the first choice because of security concerns. It was not the second choice either. Eventually, everyone did agree that it would be the fourth.

The Conferences had been sponsored for an international collection of scientists to ponder the perils of a world trying to decide its own fate. Pugwash offered a secluded location, warm hospitality and beautiful weather. It also offered what most nations could not and that was the Freedom of Thought.

In March of 1954, there had been a nuclear test at Bikini Atoll; the results of which had brought every scientist in the world to their senses, at least those with compassion, forethought and being well informed.

Doctor Joseph Rotblatt in London, England had made some very accurate observations of the radiation fall-out while other scientists became worried that the nuclear test performed by Dr. Graves had gone astray with too much radiation contamination. Supported by the Russel-Einstein Manifesto, Pugwash became synonymous with peace for all humanity.

I hadn't been born in Pugwash, but had grown up with more time spent at the conferences than most scientists. I ran errands, supplied local lobster and assisted in the care of the lawn & gardens surrounding the buildings. I was very intuitive in what staff needed for these conferences.

There was also another factor which had influenced me; this was the flow of information. I listened to everything for two months from July to the end of August; I was an unknown student. By the time I was ten years old, I knew about nuclear fall-out, radiation and other instruments of fear. I learned about governments, near and far. I understood peacemaking and dialogue; sometimes as much as Ambassadors. I saw people for what they were, not what they seemed or portrayed; at least I believed that.

From the age of six until I turned thirteen, there was no mistaking my presence when it came to the Peace Conferences. Returning participants would say hello and new ones were always quickly introduced to the staff/volunteers who sorted out the guests. On more than one occasion, I would take a small group on a tour of the harbor in one of my father's fishing boats on those quiet afternoons and early evenings. You can always see more

from the water than you could from the land, or so I was
taught.

Many people attended these conferences, some as
important dignitaries and others for religious and political
concern for the world's welfare. This was the era of
American/Soviet argument. Blame and deceit fueled the
distrust where good could be masked by bad and vice
versa. The first cosmonaut came to visit along with
representatives from the Soviet Bloc countries. There were
others that came who were too private to mention with
their own details; lots of details.

There were never any arguments, just different
points of view always accompanied with a calm
atmosphere of tolerance and open mindedness. The
newspapers and television were reporting one thing, but
in Pugwash, Americans, Chinese, Russian and others would
sit and share their concerns as a united group. This was
how I spent my summers. It was how I understood human
nature; that would change over the years after the
memory loss. Then there was my family.

My father was a very unusual man to say the least.
To the casual observer, his history was contrary to what
most would believe and his image would be just an
illusion. My brothers and sister almost had me convinced
that I had imagined this father/son relationship. I can
assume that the trust between him and me was greater
than that of the others. This would explain why I had been
brought into the unofficial club at a very early age through

an experience which shaped my life. It would create the model for the respect I would hold towards the living and the dead; the latter being somewhat more trustworthy.

On July 1st, the lobster season would come to an end. The lobster traps and boats would be hauled out of the water and stored away. The government contractors would come to dredge the harbor. I had pestered dad to take me a long on those dredging tugs and barges which would appear every few years.

The Provincial government would contract out to marine dredging companies to deepen and widen the channel so ocean going vessels could safely enter and exit the harbor without running aground. Ships from all around the world would come to pick up pulpwood, refined salt in bags, bulk coarse salt and lumber. Pugwash was the name given by the Micmac tribe to which meant "Deep Water" to some and shallow water to others. I always felt that it was in the interpretation of when and how anyone arrived depending on the tides, not in the translation.

It was July of 1962 when lobster season had come to an end that dredging once again became the local pastime for residents to observe. My father had finally given in to the notion that I would at least have to spend one day with him at work on the tugs. He came home from the salt mines one morning where he was a night watchman deep below in the tunnels. Having worked all night, he felt it would be perfect to take me to his day job. His work on a shuttle tug monitoring the engine room, handling the cables, ropes and lines for the barges was a benefit from our Government representative.

This was to be the day where the only moving would be repositioning the dredge to a new site which would require little or no activity. It would allow me to watch firsthand the wonders of tugboats, but of course, schedules do change. Upon arriving at the commercial wharf, there was a discussion going on at the temporary office which reminded me of an aluminum box on wheels. Three men in hard hats, plus two other gentlemen were in deep discussion as my father got out of the truck and walked over to them. He made it very clear that I was to remain in the truck until he motioned for me to join him.

There was some hand motioning plus some stares toward my position. Dad began having his turn in the conversation. Soon after, I was called over to join him. I thought I was going to be told to go home, as that was only a few blocks away. Only my pride would have been hurt that day, not my feet. There was a smile on his face as we approached each other.

"I do not want you to get in the way of the workmen and under no circumstances are you to bother the men who will be entering and exiting the water today," said my dad with a smile ear to ear.

My eyes grew big. The excitement which had to have been on my face was enough to reassure him that I would do exactly as I was told.

As we made our way down the dockside ladder, I could not believe my good fortune this day; I was entering a strange and wonderful place which would stay in my memory for the remainder of my life. Ironic, that these same memories would provide the catalyst to become my future reality. I remember quite vividly that I could not stop humming as if to grasp the correct tone.

Instead of the small shuttle tug which I thought we were boarding, we walked across it. There was a larger tug tied next to it, yet we crossed that one too. Finally, there was another vessel, but it had some kind of contraption on its stern with winches mounted just above the platform.

We made our way onto its deck when I heard this loud voice say to us, "Hey Kenny, what have you got there today? Are you thinking on taking a nap in the engine room while we're down on the bottom and have this lad do your work?"

There was laughter from every part of the boat where heads popped out of hatches and compartments.

My Dad just laughed and shouted back at the burly man in faded coveralls; "actually, I thought Steamboat might need a replacement for you as you never seem to find what you are looking for."

Laughter broke out once again. I focused on the man sitting on his butt with dad glaring at him and vice versa. Some things need explaining here as "Steamboat" was the nickname given to the contractor who ran most of these marine operations. He was huge! Dad and Steamboat got a long quite well. On more than one occasion, Steamboat would call him on short notice to fix some piece of equipment that his own mechanics could not repair. As for the diver, he and dad were friends since they had returned from overseas at the end of the war. Jack had been a demolition expert participating in Operation Deadlight. Deadlight was the final operation of World War 2 that would send most of Germany's U-boats to the bottom of the ocean in a predetermined place. It had been carried out by the British on behalf of all Allied nations. As much as they acted like enemies, they were not.

That was how I made my entrance that day and dad just smiled. "Remember what I said, don't bother the men!"

I was placed in the capable hands of the cook who shuffled me over to a chair in the galley. The occasional comment would catch my attention as men passed through one hatch and out the other. Taking a short cut through the galley was the easiest method to get from one side of the boat to the other when on deck.

"Hey kid, watch out for the cook. Last time we left someone in here, he turned up in the stew!"

It had to have been the look on my face, but the cook eased the apparent tension with the appearance of a bottle of coca cola and a chocolate bar. Must be a boat load of jokesters, I thought to myself as the engine came to life. The metal floor beneath me was vibrating while the bottle of coke danced across the table in front of me. I would look out the porthole every once in a while to see the harbor channel buoys passing by; the Pugwash Point lighthouse faded into the distance.

A few hours later, the engine slowed and I was allowed to go out on deck and witness a working dive platform in operation. Men who were once in coveralls were now wearing black rubber suits with two cylinder tanks strapped to their backs, hoses on both sides of their heads with a mouthpiece hanging on their chests.

"Listen guys" said the dive master, "the current will be moving pretty fast down there on the bottom in the next hour, so be careful."

Everybody was touching each other's equipment as they were watching for the thumbs up stance. Not much was being said, but there was a lot of action taking place on the deck.

"Hey Jack, where's your map?"

The big burley guy wasn't smiling anymore, just this deadly serious look.

"Hey kid, do me a favor. Run and get the map out of my locker, it's the one with the pretty girl picture on it."

I ran forward to the storage locker; the place where dad had shown me when we first arrived. Upon opening it, I looked in at a world of diving masks, swim fins, tanks, rubber suits, weight belts, lines and hose all hanging from shelving and hangars attached to the ceiling. I opened the locker with the girl on it with a butt pointing towards me. There was one hand on the waist and the other hand on one cheek. I was knocked backward as a huge blow up doll exited taking me with it right back on my butt. I picked myself up pushing aside a huge balloon in the shape of a woman. It had pinned me for that brief moment scaring the daylights right out of me. On the shelf was the map wrapped with some personal stuff including a wallet, watch and chain. I grabbed the map, closed the locker and out the hatch I went forgetting to put the blow up doll back in from where it came. I ran back to where Jack was now sitting and handed it to him looking for some kind of approval and thanks.

"Thanks kid, you didn't scare my girlfriend, did you?"

I didn't know what to think, but having two brothers who were terrors when it came to practical jokes, I responded with; "No sir, I did not," I said with an abrupt defiance in my voice; "she is one butt ugly lady!"

There was a smile with lots of laughter - though I didn't see the humor in what had happened; I passed the unofficial test. I had met a trophy wife, someone to keep the boys laughing and female company at hand. Of course, they all had been in on it, even my father. I spent the next twenty minutes watching the men checking their gear, tapping each other on the back and finally watching them fall backwards over the fantail; this served as the diving platform. It was controlled by winches which raised or lowered it to fit the needs of underwater operations of this deep water vessel. After a while, I headed forward to the communication compartment just below the wheelhouse and overheard the constant chatter coming from the men below. Water phones are the best way I could explain how anyone could communicate underwater to the surface or between each other for that fact. I had assumed hand signals were the only method.

That's how I spent the day. I was up on deck with the workers, a few times down in the engine room and the rest of the time in the galley. I found myself going back to the diving locker and looking over all the gear, trying on masks and imagining myself down below the water.

I remembered diving off the wharf and swimming along the bottom until my breath would give out and I would be forced to surface. This equipment would keep me down for hours and I could catch all the crabs and lobsters. It never occurred to me just how complicated this profession was and the many dangers that came with it.

Just then, I was brought out of my daydreaming by the sounds of an alarm. Men were running and I got scared. For a moment, I thought I had caused the commotion by coming into the diver's locker without permission, but something else was happening on the platform. It would be another thirty minutes before the divers would return while in the meantime, more divers had arrived on another vessel and had submerged in full gear.

No one noticed me as I watched from the upper winch position with a clear view of everything. Divers were trying to save one of their buddies. I will never forget the way the men surfaced that day with a body in tow.

Jack (that wasn't his real name) was gently lifted up by the make shift crane over the fantail. Blood had been oozing from the mask and the body was lifeless, arms dangling from its side. The hoses and mouthpiece were gone and in its place was some kind of strange mechanism.

I felt a hand on my shoulder and a voice spoke; "This isn't the place for a boy anymore, there's been an accident and Jack didn't make it."

I turned my head to see my father standing on the ladder behind me. I said; "What happened?" There was a pause.

"He got into trouble and couldn't find his way out which looks like he just ran out of air, poor bastard!"

I was taken back to the galley where I sat in silence until I heard the vibration and sounds of the vessel underway, probably heading back home. I got up from where I was sitting. I left the galley to go back to the stern where Jack's body was covered up by a canvas tarpaulin. It just didn't look right to me, so I pulled the cover from his face and chest.

I just stared, as this was the first time I had seen someone dead up close. I wasn't scared or sick. Of course, I had seen other bodies taken from the water, but they were usually found days later with parts of their faces missing. I was never any closer than a hundred feet from where they would be recovered from.

Here I was and as morbid as it now seems, I just couldn't stop staring at his lifeless eyes. No one had closed them. Without thought, I touched the skin on his hand and found it so cold and rubbery. That's where my dad found me that day, just sitting.

"Son, you need to come with me now. We will be docking soon and best you are out of sight because these guys like their privacy."

Doctor Vod was waiting at the fisherman's dock and pronounced the diver's death as an accident while his friends lifted his lifeless body onto the dock and into the waiting van. Having done that, the boat left there and returned back to the public wharf tying up next to the barges of the JP Porter Company painted on their side.

My dad came up from the engine room and very quietly held my hand as we climbed over the barge onto the wharf. It was silent in the truck that day except for the sound of shifting gears and road noise; not much was said.

Instead of going home though which should have taken only a few minutes, he turned right instead of left straight out of town from the wharf's entrance.

"Son, you know what happened today? It's very important that you do not mention any of this to anyone including your mother."

I nodded my head and sat there in silence for a while longer. "Dad, is Jack in heaven?"

What seemed a long time, he finally said; "There are many places he might be right now and if I had to guess, he is exactly where he wants to be. If that is heaven, then he is already there."

It was supper time before I spoke again and seated around the table were my two brothers, sister, mom and dad at the head of the table. Mom was talking about customer gossip as she processed grocery orders at the IGA where she worked six days a week.

"Dad, how come you don't go to the beach and swim with us?"

There wasn't time for silence as my mother quickly responded that he could not swim.

"If he were to ever fall overboard, he would drown and you kids would have to live in Holland with your grandparents!"

My brothers were in the midst of laughing when the moving to Holland comment silenced everyone. Not so funny anymore. Kenneth, my dad was tough, but not so tough as to forget that it was he who honed our evasion skills.

We all knew when our father got mad at my brothers, they would take off running. If they couldn't outrun him, they would head for the water. That never made sense to me as I knew if he couldn't catch you, he sure could hit us with anything that appeared in his hands. That was his character and many of the men's townsfolk had nicknamed him Popeye. It was not for the strength of eating spinach, but more so if he got mad at you.

Dad then spoke and quietly said; "I've been a fisherman the most part of my life and never learned to swim. Now, I'm just too old."

He mentioned his crossing from England to France during the War and his greatest fear was never a German bullet, but that of drowning exiting the boat. It was hard to visualize a soldier with a rifle on his back, a bicycle beside him walking down the gang plank from a Troop Transport. But that is the way his mechanized group reached European soil.

Water scared the hell out of him. I guess everyone failed to remind him that Pugwash meant that term exactly; "Deep Water".

Besides, he said; "I know some divers without their rubber suits and tanks would sink to the bottom too."

I could not visualize that statement but in the years that followed, I did learn that some of the old clearance divers never learned to swim; imagine that!

The next morning, I gathered up some bricks and rope as I headed for the beach where I designed my own weight belt. I'd walk out into the water until my head submerged. I found walking wasn't as easy underwater as it was above even with twenty pounds of brick wrapped around my torso like a bandolier of ammo.

For days I would gather up garden hoses in which to breathe from, even trying one of the huge glass jars which were used for shipping pickled fish. It wasn't bad to see through when under the water but it would take two hands to hold it in place. I would pop back to the surface like a cork.

It was a summer of experimenting. There was much laughter directed at me by the other kids. They would take delight at watching some pretty stupid endeavors to remain under the water. By the end of the summer though, I learned to hold my breath for over a minute and made extra money from the local fishermen taking ropes from their propeller shafts whenever they got caught in the lobster lines.

I explored the harbor channel and found many things that people had thrown away over the years from wood stoves to automobiles; what fun I had! But there were those times when I would without thought, think about that dead diver. I felt a kinship to him as well as the boat which had brought us ashore.

The summer came and went. School filled my winter. Soon, Christmas was upon us and it was on that day the thought of diving re-entered my mind as I opened gifts. Dad had just come back in from the attached woodshed to our house and handed me a last gift. It was implied that the Great Lobster God wanted me to see things clearer in the future. I could not understand the point he was trying to make, but a gift is a gift no matter whom or where it comes from. Christmas was about generosity.

"Here son, this must be for you."

Hurriedly, I took it from his hand and tore the wrapping paper away to find a diving mask with fins and a snorkel. I looked up and saw that my father was now smiling with a wink directed only at me. Those were the early years and though my father passed away just after my fifteenth birthday, he was never able to see what I had become. His rule about secrets would prove so right in the years that followed. I would follow his advice right down to a T.

"Son, secrets are for good reasons and in the case of Jack, no one would have understood even though you wanted to say what happened that day. These are the rules and you will learn as the years go by the reasons why. When you are old and gray like your dad, then you can tell whomever you want."

I nodded my head.

"Son, don't say one word to your brothers, but most of all, not one word to your Mother."

2

The Defining Moment

It was on my 14th birthday that my Father informed me that I was old enough to fish lobsters on my own. The spring season had already begun and he was utilizing his fishing license for those two months. I was just finishing up Grade 8 at Pugwash District High School and the thought of fishing on my own was rather exciting; I was becoming a man.

I would be fishing the fall season in another district with the same fishing boat that both my brothers had begun their careers in and the first one my father had built for himself. The boat was forty feet long with a V-stern that had been long outdated by the newer styles. An old six cylinder gas engine for power, a tiller stick to steer with; mounted on the port side of the boat all within in reach of the gear shift and trap hauler. What more did you need to fish lobsters?

I finished school in June of 1968 and had a few days before I would have to help out landing the lobster traps at the end of the season which coincided with Canada's birthday on July 1st. What a celebration our little village would put on with "The Gathering of the Clans" as the theme. There were Scottish games, lobster boat races, beauty contests, Highland dancing and entertainment that would last all day. It was the day that we would exercise our family tradition and win the lobster boat races. By 1968, the competition was getting pretty heavy with newer boats and more powerful engines.

The Peace Conferences had been scaled back by then and my interest in attending those events was overshadowed by a 14 year old blonde/ blue eyed summer beach resident who gave me goose bumps. We spent that summer in bliss when I wasn't working on the lobster traps for the start of the fall fishing season. It began on August 10th and would last until October 10th. For two months, I would be the master and lander of the lobsters that would be foraging the rocky bottom of District 8a in the Northumberland Strait.

The traps had to be repaired then dipped in red lead paint to protect the wood from two harsh months on the bottom. It would require a lot of my summer time along with prepping the boat. Dad would accompany me through every endeavor so there would be no mistakes or something else that I might have overlooked. The bond that was formed between him and me that summer was never to be broken, but I did forget.

Canada Fisheries allowed a trap limit of 250 pots and the day I received my official license, it was a celebration. I had my first quart of Moosehead beer the afternoon of the boat launching from behind the Canadian Legion where most boats were kept during off seasons. I can remember seeing as many as 30 boats in there at one time, some for repairs and others for storage. It was quite a sight as I grew up in the fishing industry.

My boat was hauled down to the water's edge at near low tide along with several others that had been prepped for the water. The boats had been sitting upright on their keels, some with 45 gallon drums standing on each side to support them. Bottoms were painted and engines made ready while others had pieces of lumber wedged in for added support. The local farmer would pull into the field with his tractor and wait for each boat owner to signal that his boat was ready for the water. A line would be rigged with one end attached to the keel that would pull it down to the shore line.

My turn came and I signaled that I was ready with my tow line in hand. Twenty minutes later, my boat looked like a beached whale lying out on the sand bar waiting for the tide to come in. It was a special time for me as the tide slowly came in to float my newest prize possession. The boat had been transferred into my name on my birthday as a gift to my manhood, but more so that there would not be a conflict of interest or the hint that Dad might be trying to fish two seasons which were not allowed.

I slowly watched as other boats began to float in the water. But mine was not taking on that bounce which would indicate that the water was lifting rather than filling the boat. I walked out into the water to take a look into the hull and saw water was seeping through every crack of wood. I was frantic. But before I could sound the alarm that my boat needed hauling back out, a hand touched my shoulder. A reassuring voice subdued the fear that was building within me.

"Son, relax. This boat has done that since the first year I put it in the water back in 54'. It will seal itself."

None of this made sense to me, but the trust between him and me was much greater than any fear that could be manifested by what I might have thought. I turned and looked at him. There was just a smile on his face.

"Dad, what if the water fills her up before she floats?"

I had no idea that this was to be my rite of passage. That was how we were tested as to the sea worthiness of our craft. My father raised his hand and men started moving out from the shore where all had been indulging in beer that afternoon.

Slowly, each side of the boat felt the grasp of a dozen men's hands on its washboards, slowly standing her back up on its keel. When she was perfectly balanced, the steel drums were inserted on each side with old rubber tires resting between the hull and the drums so as not to damage the wooden sides. Two men grabbed each of my arms throwing me up into the boat where I was now watching the water slowly seeping through the planks.

Suddenly, there was a bang behind me as I turned around to see what it was - a five gallon metal can was rolling across the deck towards me.

"Son, pull up the floor boards and start bailing the water out as it is coming in: Now!"

And with that said; I bailed well into the evening. An anchor had been placed at the stern of each boat as they were launched so they would not float away when the tide came in. My boat was still taking on water, but at least it had slowed down enough so I could keep up with it; it was now floating.

As other men were rowing out in their skiffs to board their boats, I could detect the sound of engines all around me coming to life. What a tradition! The anchors would be recovered while off in the darkness, each boat motored away until the silence once again covered the environment.

I realized that I had no battery to start the engine and for a few moments, I thought I would be spending the night alone. Off in the distance, I could hear a boat approaching out of the darkness. It was the old man's newest boat. I could see my father's image in the moon light as it pulled up next to me.

"How's it going son?"

I felt like my arms would fall off. My back was aching from bending over scooping the water from within and throwing it overboard. All I could say was: "This is no fun." And with that he laughed, laughed and laughed.

"Next season son, I will show you how to tighten her up while she's still on land by filling her with a water hose. The wood swells inside out just as well from outside in. When the boat hits the water, there are no more leaks."

It all made sense to me now; the lesson I should have learned was common sense. He wanted me to think for myself, but I in turn trusted him to know exactly what to do. I would have to learn to out think my own dad and spare any future laughter from the other fishermen for not figuring out the magic of the wood when it came to the water.

"Water to water son, that's the way it is done and never ever forget that;" and I never did again.

Everything else about the start of the lobster season was routine for the most part. My helper was a six foot six giant weighing in at 250 pounds. I knew it was dad's idea to make sure I was in good hands with a tough crowd out on the Strait. It was exhausting work hauling large lobster traps over the side but I managed okay. My helper's name was Boxford and he kept me on the straight and narrow. He fished lobsters during the spring season with dad so he knew every routine. I am quite sure he gave the old man daily updates on my fishing abilities.

By August 12th, I had all my traps in the water and began hauling the first ones I had set on the 10th. Needless to say that first day, I wasn't quite sure if I was a crab boat or a lobster boat. I had set my first 100 traps on muddy bottom which was crab territory and I learned another valuable lesson that day.

"Check the bottom first." This was a time before depth sounders could read that far below the water without a lot of expensive equipment. I had to learn in a hurry how to sound the bottom with a rope and iron weight. By dragging the iron across the bottom while holding the line in your hand, it was easy to interpret rock from sand and sand from rock. It took a few days, but I was starting to catch lobsters and fewer crabs.

Of course, my Dad took a job with the local lobster buyer. He would head out every day to the fishing grounds to buy lobsters from any interested fishermen. He would anchor far enough off shore and fly the "cash for catch flag" which provided some fishermen with the extra cash with no questions asked. It was legal but it did cause controversy for some boat owners who had hired others to fish for them. All lobsters were owned by the owners of the boat and of course all lobsters caught were to be brought ashore for proper tally. People needed to survive.

In the meantime, it gave my father a chance to reestablish old friendships from the war years and every once in a while, some guys would spend the day with him on the water. They always brought their diving gear though and no one seemed to mind, least of all me. I felt he was watching over me just in case I got into trouble out on the water.

August went by fast with the first day of school upon me just after Labor Day. Grade 9 would be a challenge for sure, but I figured I could balance my time at school during the day and fishing right after school. With my books in hand, I would pedal my bike down to the wharf where the old man would be waiting with the boat engine running all fuelled and bait onboard. I would throw my bike into the back of the truck and my books in the cab and down the ladder I would go. That was our routine from Monday to Friday with Saturdays being the day I had to haul and bait 250 traps.

It was hard work but I had very little maintenance to do which maximized my time on the water. I would haul a hundred traps everyday weather permitting and make it back to port just before dark. The old man would be waiting to take care of my catch then send me home to study. There would be no after school sports, no dates and no fun until the season was over on October 10th which seemed so far away.

My mom thought it was too much for me but Dad would reassure her that I was doing alright and I was. Sundays were my catch up day for school projects and most teachers knew that the children of fishermen and farmers had other responsibilities besides achieving high grades on their subjects. There was a level of toleration by all. We did our best with the time we had to study, and the teachers would give us a lot of leeway. Growing up so far had been the best time of my life. But that was about to change.

Near the end of September, dad and his friends began to spend more time on the water. In the meantime, a lot of fishermen began landing their traps early because of the lack of lobsters and the high cost of bait and fuel. There were fewer lobster buoys on the water and fewer boats making the trips back and forth to the fishing grounds. I started landing 20 traps a day before the end of September until I had only a hundred traps remaining in the water. It was getting easier to get my school work done on time and I would only fish every second day. By now, I had no helper and my body was being molded into all muscle with very little fat.

One day, which I believe was a Saturday, I left the dock as usual in my boat with the old man trailing behind me in his with some friends. He had told me to follow him once we left the outer harbor and to pay attention to his signals. It was all so mysterious. I did have a feeling that I was about to relive an old experience that I had had with him on that diving boat so many years before.

There was a fog bank way off to the northeast in the direction we were heading and just before arriving to its edge, the old man signaled for me to cut my engine. As I did, he pulled up next to me while a couple of the guys jumped over on my boat throwing the anchor line over to his. I was being set up to be towed. Before I could say anything, dad cut his engine and explained that it would be better if I was towed so we would not be separated in the fog ahead or ram into each other. Without radar, this was probably the most logical way to get where we were heading. I trusted him completely.

I was towed for about an hour carefully steering into the wake which his boat was leaving behind. I realized how easy it would have been to run into his stern without the tow line attached. When he slowed, the line would drop into the water; I would step on the clutch and put the engine in reverse, just enough to keep the tow line out straight.

The fog was thick and the air was cool. Every now and then, there would be flashes all around us and the rain would come down hard, sometimes so hard it would sting my face: then it just stopped - so did the boats as the engines were cut. One of the men in dad's boat pulled up the slack from the tow line until both boats were side by side.

The water was calm as the fog began to lift. I began to glimpse an object just off our starboard bow. I was so confused. The object looked like one of those big mooring balls that you would see in larger harbors for commercial vessels to tie up to, but out here, I had never seen such a thing.

There was a lot of commotion in dad's boat as containers and bags were opened and men busily doing things that only they had planned on doing that day. I was a bystander in something that my father had been working on these last several weeks. The mechanics of it were brilliant and the secrecy from which all of this had been carried out was astounding. I had been out here almost every day suspecting none of this had been going on.

Both boats were now lashed together and getting a peak in the bow of the old man's boat, I noticed several metal barrels each attached with a heavy rope harness. In bags were heavy lines, cable and fittings. There was so much equipment yet I never knew any of this stuff had been put onboard his boat.

Thinking about it, he did mention he had to beach his boat the night before to get some rope off his propeller up the Pugwash River. You could beach your boat on the mud flats under power and the hull would slide right up out of the water exposing the propeller and shaft. It made it pretty easy for removing ropes that would get fouled on the shaft. The tide would come in, refloat the boat and you would be back in business. But the business which sent his boat up the river was about loading rather than untangling with no one the wiser.

We moved in unison over to the mooring ball where a line was attached to keep our boats from any further drifting in the current. Something was on the bottom which my father apparently wanted on the surface.

There were two heavy lines attached to each end of the ball with large steel eye hooks. One rope was then attached to his boat and the other line was attached to my stern. The cables had been looped around both our stern posts allowing a loop to be where each eye hook was attached. My father shouted that two men would be in the water with the barrels that were just put over the side of his boat. Each one of us would maneuver our boats into the opposite direction, thus lifting whatever was down below to a point that the other barrels could be attached. It didn't make sense to me, but either did the building of the pyramids. It is something you have to witness to understand the simplicity of physics.

With both lines attached, each boat stern to stern, divers and barrels in the water, we both began to power our engines. Ever so gently at first until the mooring ball began going under the water. The distance between our sterns became greater while the old man would signal with his hands when he wanted me to increase the power and when to let off the throttle.

I would suppose that the depth of the water would dictate how far apart we would be when the thing beneath us reached the surface. Whatever it was, the huge mooring ball was mostly under water until the divers signaled that the object was near the surface. Sure as sugar, what we were pulling on was passing through some sort of underwater pulley system allowing it to be lifted from the bottom of the ocean by just the power of two boats without the need for cranes or winches. Amazing!

Each diver would disappear for a few minutes and then would reappear only to grab another barrel rope and submerge again. It must have taken a half hour before the signal was to throttle down and begin to recover the tow line that had been attached to my stern. All the barrels were now partially submerged as they began to support the weight of whatever it was they were now holding. I finally understood his meaning that you could see things better from the water than you could from the land; absolutely brilliant.

I had almost pulled in every bit of the tow line when one of the divers motioned me to throw the end that had been attached to my stern into the other boat, which I did. The excitement of what was below was starting to get to me but was soon extinguished by my father's voice.

"Son, I want you to keep a south west heading on your compass and head home. You will break through the fog eventually and when you do, the lighthouse should be on your portside. Watch the reef but if the fog doesn't clear, in exactly one hour, shut your engine down and listen for the fog horn from the lighthouse. You know the rest."

I couldn't believe my ears. I wasn't going to see the result of our endeavor or at least mine anyway. Feeling a bit slighted, I knew not to challenge the old man or whine about what he had just told me.

The tow line had been hauled from my boat. The cable had been removed from my stern post and thrown into his boat as well. I stepped on the clutch placing the stick shift into gear and started the turn away from them. I did notice that the tide had reversed direction. It was now coming in which would make my trip go a little faster. I would have to allow for that just in case I couldn't get out of the fog.

I was bit more cautious than usual and would shut the engine down every once in a while to see if I could hear the clang of the harbor buoys or the sound of the fog horn at the entrance to Pugwash Harbor. It would be a couple of hours before I exited the fog right at the entrance to the harbor. I had hit it right on.

Now my thoughts were back on what I had just left, but as much as I wanted to know more, I also knew the lessons dad had taught us growing up. It was none of my business. As I entered the harbor, I remembered my father telling me to haul a couple of strings of lobster traps that I had set just inside the harbor a day earlier. The plan was to leave them for a few day set, but he must have had a reason. I hooked the first buoy and started hauling the five traps that were attached to the line. The first trap came up fast and to my amazement; there were a dozen lobsters in it. There was just as many in the others as I hauled them up one by one.

I hauled two strings in which were tied ten traps every twenty feet apart - I retrieved almost a hundred lobsters. I could have fished all day and never had caught that many, so it was a good day after all. Actually, the old fellow had probably loaded my traps with lobsters so I would appear as to fishing the whole day, instead of helping out on his little project.

I entered the inner harbor pulling up to the National Sea Products dock and offloaded my lobsters so they could be weighed and separated. There were a lot of curious faces looking around and a few questions on what bottom I had found such good luck. I was cautious in not saying too much, but I had been gone all day.

I quickly said, "I had some traps on broken bottom that finally paid off, but I hauled over a hundred fifty for this."

Having said that, there were no more questions; I never volunteered anything else. I was the last fishing boat in for the day so the dock could be shut down for the week-end. I moved my boat over to the fisherman's wharf, tied her up and walked home through the woods. I would clean the boat in the morning after church.

By the time I got home; I call it home only because it was really the old local hospital. My parents had purchased it in 1967 to turn it into a tourist home for the occasional people who needed lodging on the Sunrise Trail.

Having tried that, it was soon adapted into a retirement home. It was profitable but a lot of work. It was huge. With 13 bedrooms, an elevator, 5 bathrooms and so much more, I was the envy of all my friends. It was almost a dream come true for a boy who grew up too fast. We even had a dynamo for emergency power if the municipal lighting went out because of storms or accident. Not only did I have my own bedroom, I had a whole wing to live in until my brother came home to visit. He never stayed too long and went back to stay with the other brother in Ontario soon afterward.

I ended my evening having supper with Mom in the back kitchen before going off to bed. I woke up to the sound of men's voices well after midnight which finally reassured me that dad had made it home safely. There was a lot of noise out there in the dark, but experience had taught me to mind my own business unless he called for me to appear.

3

Winter of 69'

It had been a long winter. I was still working on getting my grades back up to what had been expected of me. I crammed the winter with every sport I could participate in; we as a team excelled in everything. There was soccer, basketball, swimming, wrestling and cross country running. I had been late joining up but as soon as the lobster season came to an end, I hit the ground running so to speak. If it wasn't sports, then there was the work back at the retirement home with a wonderful group of disabled senior residents.

The long winter days were either filled with study, sports or resident care. On the main floor, we had five elderly adults and everything about them I remember to this day. At first, I was hesitant to help out, but a long chat one evening with the old man around Christmas changed that for me. They had no family and were in the care of the County, so we became their family.

It was just before Christmas Eve that my mother brought out her accordion and we gathered the whole group in the dining hall for some music and atmosphere. Most were wheel chair bound except old Henry who was 93 that year and still banging away on an old typewriter. There was Jack who could not walk and Cecelia who was blind but her insight was cheerful. There was Bob who had a rare disease that affected his muscles and mind but never held him back from trying to sing. Last was Alma who was a kind and gentle soul. She had the shaking palsy and for the most part was very difficult to maneuver while keeping her attention. None of the staff could seem to manage her as well as dad. He had a knack with the older people in keeping them happy and well.

He called them the ones that none of the other facilities wanted because of the amount of attention they required. As for my father, he had a very simple explanation to it all.

It was December 23rd of 1968. The candles were lit, the tree was a glow and mom had the whole group sitting in a semi-circle. Dad and I were standing in back of the cafeteria without saying too much to each other. Mom began playing up a storm; even old Henry was starting to enjoy it. He was deaf as a door but the handclapping of the others, especially Cecelia, kind of brought him to life. She had an infectious way of clapping and stamping her feet to the beat of the music which reaffirmed to me that the blind were not to be pitied, just hugged and made to feel welcome.

Dad nudged me to follow him. Without thinking too much about it, I said; "What's going on?" The timing surprised me a bit.

"Son, this is what it's all about. This extended family of ours needs us as much as we need them. Even though they seem helpless and totally dependent on our assistance, they enrich us in a way that is unfathomable. What we are doing here makes us a better family. Remember that."

All I could do was nod my head and look back at our little senior group. It was then that I felt such warmth for these people; they were family.

I got the nudge to follow him and out the side door we went. Mom would be fine with the nursing assistant hovering over everyone's needs. She lived across the street from us and worked the week-ends and holiday evenings when needed. We were in the same class in school but there was no awkwardness in our situation. She was a nice girl.

Once dad and I got outside, he unlocked the door to the dynamo room where the massive generator lay silent. I was never allowed in there nor did I want to without his permission. It was an understanding that I would never challenge with good reason. I respected his authority.

The door opened and soft lights illuminated the interior. Everything was so neat which was something I was not use to seeing. The generator was spotless with benches along the sides. There was a lot of stuff hanging on the walls which I now realize came from salvage that he and friends had recovered over the years. I was amazed with the details.

"I am going to show you something, but before I do, you have to promise me that you will never speak of this; ever."

All I could do was nod my head, but my mind was racing trying to figure out what it was he was going to show me. There were two windows on one wall that he proceeded to close. The wooden shutters were covered with aluminum which I assumed was to dampen the engine noise while the generator was running. It was obvious to think along those lines until the moment a large box was pulled out from under one of the benches. It was covered by a tarpaulin which he slowly pulled off exposing something I had never seen before.

"When I open this, do not be scared or turn away from what's inside. It will not hurt you."

With that said, it did. Upon opening the lid which required all his strength, I was encased by a light which had no color. It filled the room and what happened from that moment, once the fear passed, I cannot say. I just knew. I didn't have to speak, it could hear me. His lips never moved but I heard everything it had to say. I saw what was on Dad's mind and knew then that his time above the earth was coming to an end. I'm not sure how long we stood there together, but the connection that was made would remain with me forever: this I knew.

Something in my brain had changed how I viewed things. I looked at him and him at me. I realize now he had no concept of what was in the box or the power it could manifest. I had to see what was inside.

There is no mistaking what Moses might have thought or seen. The tablets appeared more as instruction boards, yet the inscriptions were unfamiliar to me, something that would remain unknown for a long time.

The power within the dynamo room brought to mind everything I had learned in summer Christian camps. He closed the lid of the chest, but I could not close my mind. A new dimension had been introduced to me.

I would never understand the winged features upon the lid even less than the German Swastika situated between them.

"Was this the thing that had been so secretive a few months ago out on the Northumberland beneath the metal ball?"

My father was a complicated guy when it came to his faith. On more than a few occasions, he would wail out a hymn or two either with mom playing the piano or organ. He had no knowledge of this thing or its infinite purpose.

I had seen the swastikas in pictures that dad kept in his memory drawer from the War. I had also seen them in pictures that my brother had been sending home from an Air Force base in Germany where he was stationed.

I didn't know how many times he had opened this thing, but knowing him, it was probably every chance he could.

"Dad," I said. "What is it? Where did you get it?

"Son, isn't it great? I've never seen anything like it and I think it's all made of gold."

With that said, he just stood there motionless holding both hands to his temples behind his eyes. I could see he was in pain.

"Your uncle and I found it down by the brick factory a few months ago," he said - once again; "Not a word to anyone. You hear me?"

I didn't want him mad at me, but the more I thought about, I remembered the old brick cart tracks that had been cut deep into the old railroad bed. They ran from the brick factory behind our house into the backyard before the first snow fell. The weight of it had to be enormous let alone awkward. On the wall was a German Iron Cross hanging on a nail. I wanted to know more, yet it wasn't really important; I just followed him out the back door. He closed it snapping the lock on it. The image left in my mind was how to get this thing underground; this had to be done.

4

The Funeral

Spring came in 1969 like a Lion and left a lamb in its place. It was the day before April Fools' Day that we were hard at work preparing the lobster traps for yet another season. We had two licensed boats to be fished with the old man using one and someone else to fish the other. Dad's choice was hardly a wise one, but good fishermen were hard to come by and this guy had been very good. His only problem was keeping him sober but the old man knew how to do that.

Over the winter, my folks were made an offer on the Retirement Home which they finally accepted after much discussion; I was glad. They felt old and my father was experiencing severe headaches that would almost leave him blind. He would roll on the floor clutching his head with his hands. There was nothing my mother or I could do; the tumor had infiltrated into the feeling part of his brain.

It was April 1st that the first stroke caught him while he slept. We had purchased a mobile home to live in until the fishing season was over; then there would be a new home for us somewhere down on the Gulf Shore. He had mentioned it but had not related the location to me or mom; that was his way.

The stroke paralyzed his left side and just after daylight, my mother called for me to come to their bedroom to help. I knew then that the time had come. Upon entering their bedroom, she was hard at work trying to dress him. It was tough seeing him like this, but he remained somewhat silent. His eyes never left mine and I never left his. I could see a light in there, but the body was unresponsive.

It was awkward, but we got him out to the truck and drove to the Hospital. There was not much any of us could do for him now; just wait to see what the doctor would say. He was transported from Pugwash to Amherst that very same day. I realized that my school days were coming to an end.

The man who was to fish one of the boats decided he could not work for a woman and quickly found another position with someone else. That left me with having to fish back to back seasons. Was I prepared for that? I already knew that it would happen; I just didn't know when.

Mom called my older brother from Ontario asking him to take over for my dad, which he did and brought his family from to Nova Scotia on a leave of absence from his own work. Everything was becoming complicated. It would have been better to have left both boats on shore.

The start of the spring lobster season began without fanfare, but my brother was a pretty competitive guy. I had my hands full just trying to keep up with him and eventually, I just went my own way. It was four days after the start of the season on my 15th birthday that the family got the news about the old fellow that it was definitely a tumor in the brain. It was too deep to operate and remove. They gave him six months to live.

The start of my day was always on the water pulling traps until late afternoon. I had just entered the harbor when I saw our truck heading for the Fishermen's Wharf where I would be tying up the boat. Mom, my sister and not too far behind them was my brother in his Ford Cyclone; this was not a good sign.

It took me a few minutes to get the boat squared away with all the boat lines secured. Three of them were standing about ten feet over my head. What seemed like a moment of silence turned into who could give me the bad news first; I got the message but the delivery could have been better rehearsed. I had been preparing for the worst since the time I had seen it in the generator room.

What took place for the next fifteen minutes was a need by all three to somehow be the one who would tell me the bad news about dad. I kept working in the boat with no emotion or show of reaction. The last words that came from the Old Man were; "not one word, not to anyone." I understood it to apply right now. Of course, Grace was the first to blurt it out which sent Gary into the first born rage of "that knowledge was mine to share first."

Mom, for all her heart felt emotions walked back to the truck, crawled in and never said another word.

I finished washing down the boat, putting things in order all the while Grace & Gary having that family argument for everyone to hear on the wharf. Fortunately, they all left; there was no need to dwell any further upon the past. I looked around the harbor and took in every view from the brick factory to the Salt Terminal across the harbor. I knew in my being that I would be leaving this place in a few months. It was going to be a very emotional bumpy ride, but I would be back someday. I didn't know when, but I did know why.

The fishing season came to an end on July 1st 1969. Part of me had matured in ways that I would someday understand while this tiny secretive part of me had been isolated in time. I didn't want to know why and I did not care.

My mother felt I needed a vacation and as luck would have it, my aunt and uncle in Dover, Massachusetts opened their home to me with a round trip plane ticket from Halifax to Boston. The summer came and went very fast. I would be returning back to Pugwash just in time for school. Dad had been transferred to the Veteran's Hospital in Halifax for cobalt treatments which destroyed more of his brain yet did not eradicate the tumor. I went to visit him a couple of times before I left to live with my brother in Fort Erie, Ontario. Life was not fair.

I had a brother who thought he was my father and would not take no for an answer. I on the other hand rebelled, not wanting to be there anymore than he wanted me there. After a while, you get use to the beatings, but for the life of me, I never understood when he would tell me that Dad would beat him for no apparent reason. I had no other memory than a good father.

I spent the tenth grade mostly as an outsider in a city I did not fit well into. The people were nice and the winter was spent living alongside the Niagara River a few miles above Niagara Falls: my thoughts and the water were always moving.

My father passed away near the end of September at the Camp Hill Hospital. None of us were there for his final breaths and most of the family were relieved that his suffering had come to an end. I would someday return back to that same hospital to have an ear operation and be confronted by an old memory that had long been forgotten. It was the launching point that I had long waited for but never realized the connection.

Our mobile home was transported from Pugwash to Fort Erie where it was set up next to a hotel alongside a place called Frenchmen's Creek. I missed Pugwash, my friends, my family and yes, the water. I had become part of it as much as it had become part of me.

School ended in Fort Erie just after I took the driving test for my driver's license. I was no longer walking to school and evolved into a very popular guy in my judo classes. I suddenly became the guy who made sure everyone got home safe and sound. I finished school only to be swept away on a European adventure back to my mother's homeland of Holland. It was a nice summer living with my grandparents, but more so the many visits to Germany on my bicycle being very educational.

I had spent a couple of days at The Hague where the International Court of Justice held its official status. From Pugwash to Den Hague, I had not only witnessed Conferences on Peace, I became infatuated with the ideals of a World Court. This love affair would last until I arrived back on Canadian soil where I was informed that I would be leaving Ontario to live with my sister in Newfoundland. Any hope of returning back to Pugwash was extinguished with this news at first, but as luck would have it; my destiny was still waiting in Nova Scotia.

Somewhere between Ontario and Newfoundland in August of 1970, I was able to rekindle that first love I had left behind a year earlier. Time would have it that there would be no time; but time there was to be as one if only for a few days.

I was leaving for Newfoundland and she was leaving for Coco Beach, Florida. She would never see me again, but I would see her on many occasions without her knowledge. It wasn't stalking, but I did remember our last night together at the drive-in movie. We cuddled in the back seat of a car, professing our love and allowing those last precious moments to stand still forever. My last thought was from the Star Trek series; "Space, the final frontier' as our thoughts and minds became as one. It would be a day later when I opened my suitcase and found all my underwear had been sewn up at the crotch with these words; "Kilroy was here." Her mother had a sense of humor alright, but I never crossed that line. My plan of not having sex until we were married was still intact.

My sister had just completed University with a teaching job secured in Newfoundland. Now I had a sister who was determined to be my father. This was even worse than the situation I had just escaped from as she and Dad had spent many years at odds with each other. My recollection was that both their personalities held some pretty stubborn traits but they both did love me.

It was August when we finally hit the road for Newfoundland. The music on the radio was Blind Faith and my sister's new husband to be had the same name as the brother I had just left behind. I was moving to a new place that had the same name as my other brother. I knew then that I didn't have a hope in hell and even less of a one for the future.

5

Memory

Lost

Our move to St John's, Newfoundland began to unfold upon arrival at Argentia. It was just a ferry Landing; my first welcoming point to a very strange land. Off in the background, there was a naval base which was operated by Americans. It felt like such a secretive place.

There were no other signs of life as we exited through the nose of the car ferry. I wasn't very comfortable in this new land and something was trying to tell me to return from whence I came.

The next year and a half of my life was not going to be easy, but at least our family was intact or what remained of it. Grace, Mom and I were on an adventure that would change our lives forever. For mom as a new widow, this would be the place that she would find a new husband. Grace would marry a Newfoundlander and raise a family. I would forget almost everything I knew; relearn everything I didn't want to remember and never look back when I finally left. This province had been hard on me for sure, but it gave back my life in more ways than I could ever be thankful for.

I left Newfoundland on April 1st, of 1972 bound for a small village called Pugwash. I was alone with some memory and no reason why I needed to do this; I just had to leave. I purchased a one way ticket at the Argentia Ferry Terminal to Sydney, Nova Scotia with just a backpack and a smile. I did not look back nor foresee that I was returning to Nova Scotia as a much different person.

6

Pugwash Revisited

The memory that I did have: encompassed only Pugwash, its people and its purpose. I just wanted peace from an outside world that I now disliked more than loved. I wanted to be safe amongst old friends.

The ferry pulled away from dockside with just a shallow blast of its horn. There were a few hand waves from those that would remain in Argentia doing the things that they have done for years; watching the ferry come and go on its overnite voyage.

I settled myself into a cabin that I could not really afford but which I required to finally acquire some rest. I slept the whole trip until we reached the mouth of Sydney harbor where I awoke to sounds of crew members preparing for the offloading of vehicles and commerce. I hadn't undressed for bed and within a few minutes, I was standing on the gangway. The smell of Sydney filled my senses with long lost pride or was it the hint of future feelings? I had the same feeling when I left Argentia that I was having now as if I was in two places at one time. It had to be that I was overtired.

The sounds of cars and trucks drew my attention to the offloading area where a familiar face was slowly moving towards his vehicle. What were the chances that another Pugwash resident would be on the same ferry? I was going home.

I headed for the terminal where my chances of connecting to a friend were greatly increased; me just being there at the correct moment. He would pass through the doors where all transportation had to pick up their tariff sheets. I asked Brian if his destination was Pugwash and finally the look of recognition broke across his face. Brian was the Postmaster's son and a driver for Kennedy's Transport business.

"Hi Frank. I haven't seen you in a long time."

We shook hands as I began to fill him in on my last couple of years in Newfoundland.

"I just have to drop my truck off at work, then yes; I am heading home. You need a lift?"

I just nodded my head and smiled.

Pugwash had not changed; lobster season preparations were in full swing along the docks. The familiar smells were coming back to me as if I had never left in the first place. I didn't know why I came back, but what I was trying to reconnect with, I could not find. There was just something missing. In a few days, I left Pugwash heading towards another part of my past called Port Elgin in New Brunswick. It was the place that I had spent the first few years of my childhood.

Aunt Elizabeth still lived there and provided a warm bed and fond memories of another time. She was kind, informative and had my best interests at heart. It wasn't long before I found a job on a scallop dragger down in Cape Tormentine. I would spend the next several months fishing the coast of New Brunswick and Quebec for the illusive scallop that fetched a hefty price in the fishery markets. There was still something missing.

I was amongst family now and rarely left the closeness of the dragger fleet. There were those moments that things would happen which made no sense until years later remembering it as what I needed to do, but didn't know why. It wasn't until we began dragging the sea beds off Chatham, New Brunswick that mysteries began to appear.

The other crewman onboard with us was a young man named Clinton. His father ran the Carpenter's shop at the Dorchester Correction Center in Sackville, New Brunswick. Yes, of course, the town where I had been born. My mother always said that I would end up in a big house, but I always hoped it would be just like my grandparent's place. For that matter, the old Pugwash hospital had already brought that into reality.

Clinton had so many stories to tell about the inmates that were relayed to him by his father. Most were funny, but there were some tales that just never seemed believable. I never thought quality human nature could survive in such a place. It pretty well scared me straight.

Clinton and I decided one day to quit the fishing and get away from our own tyrant; the skipper of the dragger. We had made a few miles away when I decided I was going to go back and stick it out. I was glad I did.

It was September that we recovered the first human bone in one of the metal drags. Along with the first remains were the remnants of a parachute encrusted with sea mussels. Another few drags along the bottom brought up more bone pieces that I began to store beneath deck. In the next few days, I recovered enough bones to fill several scallop bags with no idea what I was going to do with them let alone whom I would tell. There had been many storms along this coast and quite frankly the bones could have belonged to any number of fishermen who had drowned yet had not been found. I was always collecting this or that while my boss never asked me to disclose what I was up to as long as I did not interfere with his fishing endeavors. I was a private person and so was he.

The week-end came and though we were many miles from Port Elgin now, this week-end was the start of school. The captain, my boss had children who would be attending thus creating the perfect moment to bring the things I had collected back to Port Elgin; the bones included. I didn't know why, but their place was in a cemetery not at the bottom of the ocean. I never figured that anyone else would be looking for those same bones either.

My Father was buried in Port Elgin at the Fernwood Cemetery; where many Trenholms had come to reside. I convinced myself that I was doing the right thing.

It was not long before I began having the dreams of flight and fancy. Something about those bones had given me strange images of flying & drowning. I would wake up in a cold sweat always fearing that something was pulling me down that I could not escape from. Years later, I would learn whose bones they were and how they got there.

I buried them somewhere in the cemetery, but to this day, I am not sure where or why. I didn't have a purpose, yet there was an unmistakable drive to place them safely in the earth.

That was how I met my first wife; at the cemetery. She had been watching my movements ever so silently. Finally, she just walked up to me at dusk as I was laying the bones to rest. It never distracted or surprised me and my only comment was to say that I was burying my favorite pet. The skull & the arm bones I laid carefully on the other bones still in their bags. Maybe it was the bones or it might just have been my destiny. She had lived most of her life across from the cemetery in her father's house. I should have known her, but could not remember until years later our connection. She spoke as if she had known me for some time; which she did. She had been a cheerleader and me as a basketball player from the winter of 68'/69'.

Though our villages were thirty miles away from each other, it did not hinder a little rivalry feeling between Pugwash and Port Elgin. My cousin had been the basketball coach from my father's side of the family.

We were married November 18 of 1972. I was seventeen years old. My best man was a guy named David. Actually, his father had fished for my father back in the gulf shore years. This allowed our friendship as 3 year olds to be recovered here in Port Elgin with little fanfare and excitement.

Bev and I moved back to Nova Scotia where I found work on an offshore fishing trawler for the winter. It was my first taste of Halifax Harbor. The air base at its mouth would hold my attention as if I had belonged there all my life. Canadian Forces Base Shearwater and I were connected in more than thought; there was a medium of sorts between us.

I had felt those same feelings back in Argentia as well as the Air Base at Chatham: that was the place where I had recovered the bones the previous year. Maybe that was not it at all. I did have a brother stationed on a Canadian Air Force Base in Europe. Family ties could possibly explain the feelings that I had been having these last several months, but I felt something much deeper. I had to be working through some experiences that probably were not mine at all but had been incorporated into my own sense of well-being.

Working on the water was all I had ever known which shared the feeling that I belonged to something much bigger than me; and it was. I was still looking for something but maybe this would bring me closer to it.

Halifax was a major seaport on the eastern seaboard. Vessels from all over the world passed through here and my choice was surely not perfect but it was a beginning. I could raise a family, enjoy my water born freedom and fill the emptiness which always seemed to be propelling me to some unknown destiny.

Winter work on the Grand Banks was cold, long and exhausting on a side trawler. Ten days out, two days in and back out to sea at first as a deckhand then up to a boson's mate. Winter fishing was tough and the fish were scarce but the friendships established here would last a lifetime. But like all things, something was moving my way in the form of another ship.

It was two am on George's Banks when one of the steel cables parted taking the arm from a seaman working the forward fish hold. The cable sliced through his flesh and bone like a hot knife passing through butter leaving what remained of the arm landing on the starboard winches before me.

The seas were huge and the wind was howling at thirty-five knots, much too strong for dragging the bottom, but necessary if we were to meet our quota of fish for this trip. Things began to happen so fast that time seemed to slow down.

In a case like this, someone has to make the decision to save the person or try saving the equipment, especially the net we were still dragging somewhere below us in 100 fathom of water. The trawler was forced sideways into the seas that were now breaking over our portside. It felt like surf flowing over the beach filling every imprint on deck. There were no heroes that night.

The sun rose that morning with all hands on deck; the nets, guide doors and cables cut away many miles behind us now. The injured man was secured and alive in the forward cable room with two of us attending him. We were able to ease the bleeding with a leather tourniquet and massive amounts of bandages. It wasn't professional emergency first aid, but it saved him from bleeding out during the night.

In Canada at that time, it was not the Coast Guard which handled such emergency distress calls; it was the Navy. Just after daylight, a gray shadow appeared on the horizon before us.

We had been steaming the last few hours for the safety of Lunenburg at about 6 knots. The vessel heading towards us still miles away took on the form of a sleek Navy Destroyer. It had probably been at sea when the captain of our trawler sent out the first distress call about our injured crewman. I had spent most of my time forward away from the bridge in the anchor compartment. My crewmate and I had little knowledge about what was going on between the two vessels in what soon needed to be done.

The next two hours were filled with personnel being transferred over to us from a Saint Laurent class warship with our crewman being transported back to them. Watching everything in silence gave me a new appreciation of the difference between peace time activity and rescue operations.

With our injured now gone and only five days into the trip, it was decided to keep steaming to the National Sea Products repair facility at Lunenburg. Our skipper was a Portuguesa with little fear of the water or its unknown elements. Catching fish was priority to him, so as we sailed on to Lunenburg, I was called to the bridge to speak with the captain. It was very quiet in the Cape Hood Wheelhouse as I closed the hatchway behind me.

"Why don't you sit in the captain's chair," he said to me; "the boat is on auto pilot: no need to touch anything."

I knew then that I would have some explaining to do for what happened after the cable block split and the warp or cable as it was called parted from the gallus. The gallus was the metal frame which could be extended to guide the cable away from the hull while trawling the bottom. I had made a split second decision down below on deck without the captain's approval. Not only did I need to give an explanation, he demanded it by the look on his face.

"How long you been fishing?" He asked without a smile.

I thought for a moment; "all my life."

There was still no smile.

"How old are you now;" came the quiet chill of a man's voice ready to strike without remorse.

The tension in the wheelhouse was rising and I was readying for a man with a temper who would or probably could not understand why I had let the remaining cable which held all the gear on the bottom free wheel right off the winch. Thousands of dollars went to the bottom that morning and whether it was my fault or not, I had made a decision without his authority.

"You know lad, I've been fishing over 40 years and have seen worst storms than this with much more damage and never had to throw away an entire trawl for the sake of anyone. He just lost an arm; nothing more and nothing less."

I was speechless. I didn't know what to say and prepared for a verbal abuse that would ultimately send me packing once we reached the dock. That did not happen.

His stare was preparing me for what was going to be said next.

"When the pulley-block parted, you should have called me on the intercom right away, but instead you left your winch position and disappeared. What the hell did you do?"

This was no time to make excuses and even worse of a time to defray the blame from myself and place it on circumstances or let on that I had been scared. I tried to explain what had happened, but there were some unanswered questions in my own mind from several hours ago.

"Cappy" I said staring straight into his eyes; "Do you know why the cable parted in the first place?"

His response came very quickly.

"We got caught on some rock formation below and the cable parted or the pulley block should have been replaced during the last refit. Metal fatigue is not uncommon while pulling tons of weight which probably included a lot of fish. You acted like a novice out there;" pointing to the deck below.

There are times to keep some information to oneself; this was one of those times that saying too much would only get me in more trouble.

I relayed what had happened minutes before the cable came apart thus allowing what followed below on deck. He sat in silence as I told him what I did and why I did it. The only response from him was to tell me to go below and get some sleep. I got off the skipper's chair and went below; I started packing my gear. I felt I would be fired from the Company on shore by what he didn't say.

By the time we reached the National Sea Product's docks, I had decided less said would be better and more would never be enough. We docked in amongst the newer stern trawlers to wait our turn for repairs. The Company representatives were not long in boarding our vessel and mustering all of us on deck. Each of us was singled out to give our description of what had happened. It was no big thing but the Safety Transportation Board had to ascertain the facts and the outcome was no one to blame.

With shore power plugged into the vessel's main distribution line, we were free to return back to Halifax from Lunenburg; transportation provided by the Company. Not much was said on the drive up the Nova Scotia coast.

We arrived late afternoon to be greeted by another representative who was waiting in the parking area with two Military Officers. The skipper and I were asked to accompany these gentlemen to the Company office in the Administration Building of NSP. I didn't think much of it at first and figured it was just a continuation of another government report that had to be filled out for diverting a naval warship to an emergency medical situation.

On our way into Lunenburg, I never knew what the skipper had reported to the Company. I did know that he was the first to be called into the office where I assumed he was being interviewed for the navy report. It lasted for an hour or so. Not long after he had left the office without even looking at me, I felt a strange sense of oh no. Finally, I was motioned into the office where brief cases, charts and a tape recorder were on the table before them. I sat in the chair opposite of the two military officers who were discussing something quite privately. The first to speak was the guy with four rings around his sleeves.

The officer said "your friend is going to be alright and is now resting in the hospital. He was a very lucky individual."

I could have agreed more under the circumstances; he wasn't in my shoes right now, I thought.

"Would you like to tell us what happened out there when the cables parted from the tow?"

This was not the time to blame anyone nor try to cover my butt because of what the skipper had thought I'd done without notifying him first; so I explained it exactly as I remembered it. I know why they interview a person as soon as possible after an incident because it is fresh in your memory just like this one.

"Sir, we had just shot away on the fly about twenty minutes before the pulley block let go. The seas were running twenty feet high and more. It was difficult to even stand on deck but I have fished in worse."

I had to explain that shooting on the fly was resetting the nets with its huge doors from a recent haul back without ever coming to a complete stop. Heads just nodded as if they already knew what I had been talking about.

It was not uncommon for a skipper to set the auto pilot during a long tow when there were no other vessels around even in the weather we had. I was the starboard winch operator which controlled the aft cable of the trawl net and door. There is an identical winch on the portside with another operator who controlled the forward cable, door and trawl; the one that parted the tow line.

I had their attention as I explained that there were five of us out on deck picking through the fish from the last trawl that had been brought onboard. We were now towing into the wind with the seas breaking over our forward port quarter which was designed to shield us as we cleaned up the fish on the starboard side. It was about two am when I first heard the winch brakes starting to slip from where they had been locked down after setting out the required length of cable to move the trawl along the bottom.

"Is that when you felt that the trawl had got caught on the bottom;" came the remark from the junior officer.

"I don't think it was the bottom that we got caught on;" I said thinking of what had happened out there. "I noticed the forward cable moving from its outer position into the hull of the boat first and our heading slowly falling off to starboard."

Everything was in slow motion at that point and when I looked down the starboard side to the gallus where another block & pulley were guiding the cable, I saw both cables almost over our stern. I had made it to my winch position at the same time the forward cable sheered through the steel block & pulley.

At this time, the cable snapped apart and like a whip flailed though the air taking one of the crewman's arms with it. We were no longer moving yet the sound of the diesel engine never changed its pitch. It felt as if we were now rolling about thirty degrees from side to side in the waves.

I released the brake on my winch just slightly to allow the cable to start rolling away to counter our loss in forward movement. There was now an arm lying on top of the cable drum right in front of me as I left my position for the stern of the boat. I knew what I had to do, but to the observations of another crew member, I had abandoned my position because of the human arm.

Questions were fired at me for hours and finally I just gave in and explained what I did in those last few moments instead of calling the skipper on the intercom asking him for permission to shear the trawl. It was the skipper's call to make.

I didn't disobey orders; I just thought saving the equipment and the boat more important. On the National Sea Product side trawlers, there were retrieving lines with cable hardware that would attach to any towing steel cable. It allowed for the cable to be manually pulled back should the winches fail in a calm ocean setting. It was all in slow motion as I attached one end of the line onto a life raft pod and the other to the trawl cable that was slowly reeling out. The hardware locked onto the cable with both cable and line flying off the end of the stern. I realized that we were now moving backwards in the seas with the starboard cable now turning our stern into the following seas. I didn't stay to see the outcome of my actions on the stern and quickly returned to the winches to sheer the spooling cable with the hydraulic cutting tool just before it reached its end.

We were now free and running with the seas when I heard the engine ease in its laboring sounds. I had never used the intercom to call the Captain and left my position without authority before I sheered the cable. There was silence now which lasted only a few moments before I was asked to leave the room but told to wait outside until called back in.

I could hear a flurry of activity behind the doors and voices speaking on a phone about ships and planes. There was the mention of an Argus or something like that.

What seemed like hours probably was only twenty minutes, but the door opened with no more casual stares of a boring but necessary interview. I was ushered back to the chair and before me lay several charts of the fishing grounds. Most I recognized from our trips back and forth to those areas over the winter months.

The officer asked; "Is there any chance you would know exactly where the trawl had been parted?"

"I think so" I said, pointing to the outer banks of the Georges which were always in question on just who owned them; Canada or the United States. Of course, this was a huge area to try to pinpoint the place where all hell broke loose that morning.

"Explain to us again why you needed to attach a line to the cable before you sheared it," said the same Officer.

Now who was fishing, I thought. My father always told me to be careful about what I say when it comes to water; "loose lips loses ships."

"I figured the Company might be able to salvage all the fishing gear at a later date if they could find it. It just made perfect sense to me to attach a retrieving line."

The officer spoke; "It wasn't your responsibility to risk yourself and other people's lives. You were all at risk because you didn't follow the rules. Your job was to call the captain and let him make any decision; that is the way it is done."

I looked down to the floor and felt the need to explain that at that very moment when the brakes on the winches started to slip before the accident, I had looked up at the wheelhouse and saw that it was empty. My instinct told me that the skipper had been caught with his pants down sitting on the toilet just aft off the bridge; but I didn't. One of us being punished was enough or so I thought.

I said to the Officers; "You weren't there, but I was. I did what I thought was in the best interest of the crew. No, I didn't call the skipper on the speaker phone, but when I saw the cable turning our stern into the waves, I did what I thought was the best thing to do under the circumstances."

The Commander stood up, looked me into my eyes and said: "Maybe you got tangled with another trawler doing the same thing as you?"

It was my turn to speak and speak I did. "Sir, I had just been up in the wheelhouse before we pulled back the last tow. There were no vessels in a fifty mile radius according to the radar scope. No lights, no images and no radio chatter from anything. We were out there alone and that is what makes for good fishing."

I said it loud enough for me to finally realize that we had been fishing in the forbidden zone.

Now it was all making sense. It wasn't the bottom we got hung up on and surely there were no other boats in the area. The only other explanation could be that we might have unknowingly entangled a submarine which would have explained a lot. But of course, they already knew that and the skipper had reluctantly forgotten to identify the area of the tragedy. My captain did not know that I had attached a retrieval line to the cable before I sheared it from the drum spool.

In the next few minutes, there were more Navy Officers coming into the room and once again I was asked to wait outside. I was soon given permission to leave and head home. It was very late and with no vehicle; I called my step-father. My wife was several months pregnant and it was just too late in the night for her to drive the 30 miles to come and fetch me.

My step-dad was a great guy, him being one of two good memories I had brought back from Newfoundland; the other being his friend and neighbor from Musquodoboit Harbor. He not only rescued my mom from the clutches of that Island, he gave me a place that I could call home. He was surprised to hear my call but never the less drove the 30 miles into Halifax to pick me up. I explained that we had engine problems and the trip had been cut short. My wife Bev was waiting up for me, fat belly and all.

I awoke in the morning with a call from the office asking if I could come in and see the Vessel Maintenance

Foreman sometime during the afternoon. I had breakfast and drove back into work only to be called into the Manager's Office and made to feel very special.

"Hi Frank. I have something you might be interested in doing for the next few months. I see you lived up in Pugwash as a lobster fisherman for a few years."

I nodded my head and wondered where this was going.

"The Company has an opening for a skipper to fish one of our boats on the Gulf Shore at the McInnis Platform."

I couldn't believe my ears let alone the possibilities of going back to my roots. I didn't hesitate a minute before I accepted the offer. I would be back in Pugwash in just a few days to be getting the fishing gear ready for the May 1st opening of the spring season.

"Great," he said. "The guy up there is Bobby Trenholm. He runs the operation and will get you settled in as soon as you can be there."

I shook hands, picked up my remaining pay and headed back to Musquodoboit Harbor. Not a word of the last fishing trip was mentioned and I didn't ask. I was going home.

It took just a day to pack up the family, drop Bev off with her parents in Port Elgin and head for Pugwash. It was April 15th and I felt on top of the World as I drove the 30 miles from Port Elgin to Pugwash. Bev had some concerns which she voiced quite freely on the drive back to New Brunswick.

"Are you going back out there to look for that thing again?" she said with an increasing irritation.

"I won't," I said, but I lied. I needed to find the spot out on the Northumberland Strait that my father had brought me to so I could remember everything; the most important of which I knew I had forgot.

The drive into town brought me past the old hospital which had been our residence for a few years in South Pugwash. Next, the Alf Trenholm house that we had rented on the corner still stood overlooking the entry of the harbor. Nothing had really changed from the early years. The National Sea Product's buildings were still along the harbor between the cemetery and the house from where we once lived. It was all so emotional yet exhilarating leaving me with a somewhat eerie feeling.

I pulled up in front of the office wondering if anything had changed here in the last several years; they hadn't, the same office lady and manager were still in residence from my earlier years. I reintroduced myself and was escorted out to the storage area to pick up my fishing gear; boots and all. I signed the necessary papers and left the way I came in.

The drive out of town past the high school down the Gulf Shore Road brought back a lot of old memories of my childhood days. I had spent many a day and evening playing on those streets.

Growing up, there were three fishing camps situated down the Gulf Shore Road. The first one was the McInnis Station, the second being the Trenholm Station and the last called the Lower Gulf. They were just places overlooking the spring fishing grounds with cook-houses for the men to eat, bunk-houses to sleep and buildings where traps were stored until the next season. I had been there before, but never at the McInnis Station.

I turned off the road at my new temporary home for the next two and a half months. Bobby Trenholm was waiting there as I drove in and introduced me to the boat and traps I would be using for the lobster season. The cookhouse would serve as a meal place with a bunkhouse situated on its second floor. All the outer buildings were filled with lobster traps, ropes, buoys and everything imaginable to keep a fishing camp going for two months of the year without outside interference. There were supplies in, lobsters out, week to week from May 1st to July 1st.

In the early years, there would be as many as a dozen boats moored just inside a reef below the cookhouse. There was a road cut into the shoreline from where men, equipment and boats would make the daily route to the fishing grounds except on Sundays; the day of rest. Nothing had really changed from the first year I had joined my own parents on this coast at the age of two. The place was just a few miles down the road, but had been vacant for years. I paid it a visit within a couple of days.

The Trenholm Station was situated between the McInnis Station and the Lower Gulf Station. The name we used instead of station was called a Stand. My father's Stand was perfect as a fishing platform. Growing up, there were always four or five boats moored within the protective area behind a reef when not out fishing lobsters. These were the days when I was 2 to 5 years old; after that, the boats were sold to each fisherman with the old fellow keeping two for his own use. But I had a lot of memories here as I walked up and down the road to the shoreline. It all felt familiar. Every once in a while, I could hear the faint whisper of men singing in German; it was a language I learned while in Holland a few years before.

I made my way back to the McInnis Stand after reacquainting myself with the life we lived and the memories that came with it. The next couple of weeks went pretty fast while I learned to fish a new style of fishing with a much different boat. I remember the old fellow always commenting that the McInnis fishermen had a different way of doing things; to which I learned he was absolutely correct.

Fishing season always started at 8 AM on May 1st unless it was a Sunday; then the following day would be chosen. I left the sanctuary of the inner reef 15 minutes early that morning and was caught by the Fishery Officers who did not see the humor of my early departure. The fine was twenty eight dollars which really hurt the pocketbook. I was paid fifty cents a pound for every lobster landed which took a few days to get it paid off; lesson learned.

It was a good season the first month of May with many lobsters landed. I didn't spend any time looking for the place the old fellow called the ling hole; I saved that for the month of June. All of the other men bunked upstairs while I utilized the cook's bedroom off of the kitchen area so that I would have some privacy with my wife whenever she stayed over; which wasn't very often.

Sometimes, at least every so often, I could hear those faint whispers of men singing over the summer breezes at night always in German. There was this unmistakable feeling that it was just the wind howling through the wires so I never really paid much attention to it; until one night I felt the need to walk outside and peer over the boats now riding at anchor a few hundred feet off shore. There was a radiance of light just beyond the reef which I first attributed to the Seventh Day Adventists who maintained a summer camp next door. It was a sprawling compound of multiple buildings which could probably house more than a hundred guests at one time. It wouldn't be so odd to think that some of them might be trying to pull lobster traps at night for a feed of lobsters. I went back to bed without another thought of what I might have seen.

Five am in the morning was our usual time to have some breakfast, pack our lunches and make our way down to the shoreline. Our dinghies would be hauled down to the water's edge where each one us would make our way out to the boats. It would begin with the sound of the engines; the dropping of the mooring bridle and off we would head out to open sea with dinghy in tow. It would be left anchored just outside of the reef to be picked up again on our return. This was the routine, Monday to Saturday.

In June, I started coming in later each day to land my lobsters which did not make Bobby too happy of having to stay later just for me. He had to prepare all the lobsters at the end of the day for transport back to the factory in Shediac, New Brunswick. I tried to explain that I needed time to set my gear on better ground by using the sounding iron. He gave me a lot of leeway to the point that I could land my lobsters in the afternoon and go back out if I truly desired to increase my catch; which I did.

I needed to find that place where dad and I, along with the divers had recovered that stuff from the bottom of the strait. I knew I was close yet every day, I would keep sounding the bottom hoping for the feel of something that should not be there. The old fellow had this knack of lining objects up on shore to remember exactly where to find any kind of bottom to set his traps on. I could not quite remember what those objects were. Sometimes, it would be a cottage on the shoreline and a clump of trees somewhere far beyond it, or it would be some giant boulder on the shore and a house set way back on the land. I had almost given up on it until one day just before dark, the rope in my hand began to take on the feeling it was bouncing across metal deep down below until it was pulled out of my hand. I let go of the rope and put the engine in reverse as fast as I could until the boat came to a stop. I looked all across the water in a full circle and saw no other boats; I was alone. The current was hardly moving now as I pulled the line back until it was perpendicular to the water. Whatever my sounding iron had caught on was now directly below me. I looked landward and what I couldn't remember came back to me with everything lining up on three angles from shore.

I quickly paid out another 20 feet of line before I tied one of my buoys on it. I had no way of knowing the exact depth so I dropped another line over with a similar weight at the end of it. Somewhere below me, the weight hit something solid which sent back a vibration that it was metal below. I quickly retrieved the second line, threw the buoy over that had been tied off to the first line and headed back to the mooring area. I was contemplating a no, no which meant that I would return with diving gear the next perfect day; alone.

The old clearance divers had always told me to never, ever dive alone and if I did have that urge, not to do it without some kind of surface support. Who could I trust?

The next few days had brought a high pressure in with 10 to 15 knots of wind blowing out of the Northeast. This always made for the ocean being stirred up with little or no visibility under the water. I would check each day the spot to make sure the line hadn't chaffed off and the buoy still in place; so far so good. I had to figure a way to get some diving gear without anyone knowing what I was up to and that would not be easy. Bobby, the stand manager watched us like a hawk, not because he didn't trust us, it was that he felt responsible for each and every company boat. Finally, I decided on borrowing a boat from Pugwash instead of using my own.

I had a few friends in Amherst who were avid divers and purchasing some gear was pretty easy without a certificate. I rented a few extra tanks and planned on the day I would make a try for what I had hoped was still on the bottom. At the end of the week, the weather cleared, the tides were right and I put my plan into motion.

I borrowed a lobster boat from one of the Allen's in Pugwash for fifty bucks, loaded my gear and made my way down the gulf shore late Saturday morning. There were only a few boats out that day and no one from the McInnis Stand. I counted each boat off still on their moorings. No one would know me out here today. Just about the time I relocated the buoy, I noticed a fog bank moving up the coast towards my position. This was starting to get a bit eerie as I remembered that same sort of thing the last time I had played tag with this thing below. I dropped my anchor, shut the engine down and waited for the current to slow. I was dressed now in a half inch thick rubber suit and waiting for the moment I would have enough courage to drop over the side. I had lowered a rubber tire over the side earlier so that I would have a way to get back in the boat. My heart was racing and thoughts of what I might find were sending me into delusions of excitement. I listened for any sound of another boat engine close before I sat on the washboard and just fell over backwards into the water.

It took a while to get neutral buoyancy but I finally did. I was using the old navy regulator with the dual hoses and found it to be perfect for the job at hand. I had taken some diving courses in Newfoundland at the pool in Torbay; plus made a few dives up on the Gaspe Peninsula. I wasn't that experienced but I was not a novice either; I was just stupid for doing this alone.

I followed my anchor line down instead of the sounding iron just in case nets had been lost down below over the years. I did not want to get caught in something that I could not possibly escape from. It took me a while to reach the bottom and visibility was about 12 to 15 feet. I had lots of light from above and with my compass; I made a slow kicking movement in the direction I had planned on according to where the sounding iron had caught onto something days before.

I was having some difficulty breathing at first on the bottom, probably because of the excitement and not using the angle of my body to increase or decrease my air flow. There was a knack to using this apparatus, but once you get the feel of it, there is nothing better. I was careful as I made my way across the muddy bottom and saw no nets or traps until I saw a shadow up ahead. My sounding line was dangling from a structure almost on its side with a few other things which had been tangled in it over the years. I had found the U-boat.

I hadn't imagined those other times here in this place and surely not what the old man's little known Lion's Club had been keeping secret all those years. I swam its full length before I realized that this was all I needed to see. I would be back someday, but not alone.

The fishing season ended on July 1st of 1973. The traps were hauled and placed into storage, the boats were hauled out, engines removed and boats turned upside down. The camp was shut down, we were all paid off and everyone returned back to their homes; all except me. I rented a small cottage a few miles up the coast, almost where the folk singer Ann Murray had built her house next to the golf course a few years later. She had no idea how much history was within her grasp and I guess the rest of us really didn't care. What was important to me was the fact that I had not imagined those early years. We came back several years later to make sure that it no longer existed and for good reason. This time though, I came back as a member of the Royal Canadian Navy. Having spent four years in uniform should have prepared me for what lay ahead.

It was very difficult to see what I had searched so long and hard for a very long time proving to myself that my memories had been real. I had believed and felt so connected to what had once been inside that old submarine; it had affected the most inner parts of my being. As for Bev, her only interest had been the possibility of having some kind of gold treasure within her grasp those early years. I had not told her much, but I did talk in my sleep.

Every compartment had been explored, contents recovered right down to manuals and documents which had been well preserved in specialized containers. There was still a mystery with everything removed, but it would have to wait until I was old and gray.

U851's implosion happened on 8 am one warm August morning leaving not a trace of what it had been or even how it had got to its place of rest. It no longer existed as far as the Navy was concerned, but in my mind, it was still the same thing which had brought me back here in 1973. I was finally at peace with myself.

7

Asleep in the Deep

September 90'

Darkness invaded my consciousness as I came to rest at the water's edge of the rocks. A sharp pain was stabbing me on the forehead as each wave lifted my body dropping it in somewhat the same place. I knew what it meant as the saying goes, "Between a rock and a hard place!" However, there was a voice, a familiar voice that I had not heard in years as my mind drifted back to another period.

"She will burn you Trenholm" said the Warrant Officer standing behind a desk with no cover on his head.

I lifted my own head from where I had been supporting it with a closed hand under my chin. It was fairly easy to fall into "The Thinker" statue silhouette as I pondered my options.

I responded with "Sorry Chief, what did you say?

"She'll burn you for the sake of her own insecurity. Wives do not take kindly to change without their approval or being left alone for days, weeks and what could be years."

It took me a few moments to form words from my thoughts. "Chief, the choice I intend to make is not about her, it's about me."

I could not tell him that she wasn't my wife, just the mother of my child at this time. Naval documents and regulations are very accurate and require only married personnel to reside in Permanent Marriage Quarters. I glanced back to the window and decided less said is best right now. I looked around the room at the faces of the others, chosen by that mythical hand which pulls records, reviews backgrounds and contemplates something quite unorthodox without too many knowing the details.

Actually, I believe we all thought we were volunteering for something special. I was the only one married, the rest being single without relationships.

The Chief was being adamant about this subject. "Listen, women need someone to talk to whether it is a girlfriend or a co-worker, they will talk and you will pay the price of being discovered."

There is always some mystery to military design. There is hocusing pocus with a flair for the top secret stuff, always without a complete explanation of the consequences. That is the way it is done. The Chief had one last thing to say.

"Alright, for the rest of you knuckleheads, be back here at 1800 hours in your civilian clothes and don't forget: there is no word on this one."

From the back of the room as chairs were scraping across the brick floor we all heard, "Hey Chief, if recruiting gets slow, you could take a crack at marriage counseling!" The tension disappeared as laughter filled the hall.

I stepped out into the daylight from the underground building and felt the warmth of the sun's rays replace the damp chills of that old soundproof bunker.

From behind me came a voice. "Anybody want to meet at the Fleet Club for some suds and guts?"

A resounding yes followed from all as we headed down to the dock to catch the navy launch back across the channel to the Base.

In 1979, Halifax and Dartmouth, Nova Scotia were sister cities separated by water, joined by two bridges, three ferries and naval motor launches which traverse across on a daily basis. On the Halifax side, Canada's Atlantic Fleet of destroyers, 3 submarines, support vessels and visiting ships filled the docks and jetties. There were even more on moorings alongside HMCS Dockyard. Just above this, Canadian Forces Base Halifax stands as a guardian with many schools and clubs which make up its concrete and brick formations. Weapons School, Engineering and barracks surround the recreational areas deemed to keep the soldiers, sailors and airmen in good health and fine spirits.

The Officer's Club and the Fleet Club for the lower ranks are on each end of the base. We were just one big happy family with a good portion of the entire 86,000 personnel force which makes up the Canadian Armed Forces. This had been my home for a few years but it was not from where I had come from.

Before the Navy, I had spent a few months onboard the Oceanographic Ships across the harbor in Dartmouth and an aging naval research vessel over in Halifax. I had a nasty habit of going over the side to take a swim every chance I could and became unofficially known as the guy who loved to jump into the winter waters of Bedford Basin. There was just something about cold water that I could not resist.

Next to the container pier resided the Atlantic fishing fleet and the easy option to go to sea without training or documents. I like to believe I had tried it all but the fit never seemed right. Even now, I was searching for that something that I could not put my hand on and yet was just within my reach.

We all arrived at the Fleet Club within minutes of each other and found our usual table empty with just a folded white card on it. 'AMMO DUMP' was all it said.

This was the suds and the guts usually came after several glasses of that amber ale. Music was playing from a jute box in the corner. "Come on you, show me the way".

There were other sailors around us discussing the new fleet design and each hoping to be chosen for the "Super Stoker Program". They were the career sailors.

Canada had two classes of destroyers for her fleet, Saint Laurent & the 280 Class, the latter being the newest. The Capital Ship replacement program had been initiated to replace the aging destroyer fleet and it would require engineers of highly technical skills to augment the program. That was not our destiny.

In life as in just before death, we all have experienced that slight realization that this is familiar or I know I have been here before. It was something that most can't place their finger on, but I could.

I pushed the chair out from where I had been sitting; stood up and pulled out my wallet. A shiny new Canadian twenty dollar bill filled the void. At the bar I paid for two jugs of ale and returned hoping to see someone else liberating glasses for our table. I sat down and looked at every face. I had no idea at all who these other guys were; or their motivation. I didn't want to either.

A few months previous I had been at Canadian Forces Base Borden as a course candidate at the Physical Education & Recreational Instructors Unit. I was slim, trim and ready to take on the world as a PERI 851. There would be no need for records here or to prove otherwise.

I had been notified that a Special Program had been given the green light and it was decision time. It felt like boot camp all over again where a bond is formed that is hard to break. It had been a wonderful course. I was at the peak of my physical condition thanks to a very dedicated group of PERI's.

The exit was to be my choice but it was a difficult decision. Thumbs up was the call and in a few hours, I broke my thumb going over the pummel horse in gymnastics' class. The exit had been set and I took it. I spent the next few nights at the Barrie Hospital being fitted with a steel pin and a chip under the arm.

This was procedure. In the years to come, I would always wonder about the class and especially the good Instructors.

The older guys draw the most attention when something is in doubt.

"Hey Trenholm, what did the Chief mean when he said; there is no word on this one?"

You could hear a penny drop on our table as I said, "The word carries with it a double edge sword."

"See those guys at the table next to the bar?"

Everybody looked in unison at the supposed newest candidates for the Super Stoker program. "I think we have been chosen for a very special program, one so secret that the top brass in Ottawa have no idea of its consideration or conception. I think our future is in the sand somewhere"

With that said, there were just a few mumblings while the jute box was changing to Deep Purple's "Smoke on the Water" which sent all of us into the silent mode.

The other meaning for "The Word" needed no further explanation. There were more secrets on Canadian Ships than any other Navy. It had long been rumored that ghosts inhabited our vessels and in some cases, Aliens from outer space. My guess is just too much beer in the mess decks could make anything possible. The extra glass on the table was for that. It was an old tradition.

I looked at my watch. It was 1500 hours. There was enough time for one beer and back to the barracks to shower and change. At the base gates, a small bus was waiting to collect all fifteen and transport the group over to the other side. The 'other side' meant Dartmouth, where privacy was as accurate as any word or place. At 1800 hours, class reconvened as if we had never left at all that afternoon.

The Chief Warrant was there along with several gentlemen in suits and blazers, none of who looked civilian yet hardly resembled active or retired military. They were just different. It would be several weeks before we were informed that these men had represented the best that the FBI and the FSS could produce within the Intelligence arena. In my case, I would learn something much sooner.

They were assigned to teach us the basics of Intelligence and teach they did. Both sides of the equation had to be taught and we were the students.

"Each one of you when called will accompany one of these men for a private interview. On your desks in front of you, there are papers for each to read over and sign. You will not discuss the contents to anyone nor shall you leave this building without a final decision and commitment." This was September of 1979.

The Prime Minister was the Right Honorable Joe Clark and Allan McKinnon was the Minister of Defense. Brief as it was his tenure, the latter's experience in artillery was necessary as a basis to what lay ahead.

This was how it all began and at the end, I would know exactly what the Chief meant when he said; "She will burn you, Trenholm".

And burn she did, over and over again until I became immune to her every word and action.

The time for my interview came at midnight. All the necessary papers had been signed and I felt I was on information overload rather than lack of sleep. The room down the hall was damp and musty. There was one desk, three chairs and a banquet table at one end. On the wall was a map of the world and on the floor were three flags, Canada, NATO and the United Nations. I could not interpret the three flags as the left over era of Prime Minister Trudeau. Canada first, NATO second and UN last.

The interviewer had dull eyes, silver hair and a slight twitch when he fell into deep thought. His eyes seemed to be looking right through me as I pulled up the chair in front of the desk. On the other hand, the interviewer was as plain as the guy next door.

"Why do you want to do this?" he said in a low raspy voice. This must be the test that I had to pass, or so I thought!

"Sir, I feel like I am needed somewhere else."

There, I said it. It was not the unknowing nor the expectation that was exciting me, it was something familiar.

"First, let's set some ground rules here," he said without a smile. "Answer my questions precisely. Secondly, what you say in here shall remain between you and me. I looked right into his aging eyes and understood the look.

"You graduated out of Cornwallis with an injury. You led your class and completed every exercise. You graduated first at Boson School and Engineering School, all in that order. You were then posted to HMCS Ottawa and that is where your records went into the toilet. Is that contributing to your Country?"

I felt a shiver crawling up my back at that moment. How much does he know? I couldn't tell him that my worst nightmare had just come onboard.

"I am more interested in the World when I cannot visualize a future in my own Country." I meant it as I said it.

He got up from his chair and walked around the table until he was standing directly behind me. I could feel the icy stare of a man who had sent many others to their end. I figured he had no idea what I already knew.

"Close your eyes and tell me what I am doing right now without opening them." It was an unusual request, but why not have fun with it?

"You are deciding what to do with this Seaman at the tip of your fingers. I would like to add that it would be nice if you would stop trying to decide my future. That has already been decided or I would not be here."

I had the feeling he thought I had a chip on my shoulder; little did he know, it was in my armpit. I decided to have some fun with his lack of knowledge. It was just a guess, but I sure got his attention from that moment on. I opened my eyes as he walked back to his chair. He just sat down and stared at the table for what seemed minutes. He heard me alright, but I did not move my lips.

There was a silence as he pushed his chair back on the two rear legs and his eyes pierced into the very depth of my soul. I watched the words form on his lips.

"Tell me, what do you see right now?"

I looked into his eyes and said; "I see you as a quiet man sitting in a high rise office with cute secretaries all around you." I thought to myself, a creator and destroyer all in one; the ability to hire & fire at once. A smile cracked at the corner of his mouth as the chair came to rest on its four legs.

He said, "Tell me what the records won't say about you. Where are you from?"

My mind was flashing back to another time and place. I never wanted to leave and had no reason to stay.

"I grew up in Pugwash on the Northumberland Strait. I left when my father died and went to live with family in Ontario."

He rolled his hands to encourage more conversation.

"It says in your file that you are married, is that true?"

I knew the look on my face had given me away so I decided to come clean.

"I am married, but not to the woman in that file you hold in your hands." He smiled this time.

"I think we can dispense with that and keep this between you and me for now."

I felt as if he was toying with my emotions on one hand but I was still being invited as a kindred spirit to keep participating in the interview. The rules of a mind game are set by the Master, not the student. It may have felt like college at first, but in reality, he was setting me up for what he thought I knew and what else he could learn from my own admissions.

"Does your environment contain a future for you now in this light with me?" I was starting to feel his challenge and thought back to another time.

"Yes, it does. I feel like I have to go back in time in order to move forward where I need to be."

"And where is that?" He was speaking with more than curiosity.

I said "The Graves". Once again there was silence.

"Why?" It took a little while to put it all into words, but at the end I knew I had a beginning.

"My Dad got sick in 1969 and I had to balance going to school and fishing lobsters which left me a very tired and exhausted lad. My Mom wanted me to visit my Aunt in Boston so I could be a teenager if only for a few weeks."

My Uncle had a business just outside of Boston. I had the fortunate experience to have visited the old North

Church and a few other grave sites. I loved the City and its many hidden charms.

"It had been a rough fishing season and I had to grow up pretty fast to hold my own amongst the older fishermen. They were a tough lot. As for my uncle, he had been an Officer Candidate in the United States Submarine Service during the 2nd World War and was now a business man. He was trained for the Submarine Service but the war came to an end before his first patrol."

Casually, blue eyes just said "Is that the reason you wear dolphins on one of your uniforms?"

I must have looked like a deer in headlights. I began to squirm a bit and my mind kept racing into the past to figure out how much this man really knew about me. I had now to assume he knew most everything but I would learn much later that he had lots of photos but very little information as to my past. He was keeping me honest and leading the conversation to where he needed it to go.

He looked me straight in the eye and said: "What do you really know about Submarines?"

This was a time to clear the air. I was going to take this conversation to a place where he would show me the exit or maybe something else.

"I know a lot about Submarines, especially old German U-boats. When I was young, my Dad brought me out to one of the wrecks while he and some other divers tried to salvage the contents."

It was my first experience coming into contact with dead guys. There was no need to mention the other times.

"You realize disturbing the tomb of any submariner is a crime?" I thought about it for a minute before I answered.

"There were no bodies in the submarine, but one of the divers had an accident below and when they brought him up, I sat with the body and touched his hand on the way back ashore."

It was a strange thing to do, but I was probably seven or eight at the time. I was curious and as my father would say to me on many occasions; "curiosity killed the cat, don't let it be you."

I had never considered making a statement like this before, but the damage was done and I was now at the mercy of this man.

"Do you see your future now?" He was almost shouting at me.

"Yes, I do, the future is now in my past." A few moments passed and came, "How so?" He was now in control of the subject and I was the student once again.

"It's the place from which all things rise and death stalks every compartment. My life is compartmentalized. I am the hunted yet I am also the hunter. I have two lives, two souls, one below and the other above the water. I can harness that which comes from within." The Ottawa was proof of that the first day I stepped onboard.

He picked up a fountain pen in his hand and slowly tapped the point into the desk in front of me. His fingers slid down the length of the pen until they touched the desk. He looked up at me with those cold calculating eyes I would remember for years to come. I broke the silence.

"The Ottawa was my first official posting onboard a destroyer. As you so clearly said, the point to which my records went into the toilet. That is an error."

I decided to tell him that the Annapolis was the first ship I had been assigned to for Temporary Duty. The Ottawa had been on exercise with NATO and until she arrived back in Halifax, I was in training on day cruises & work-ups with other fleet ships. The Annapolis was a great fit for me and there were no complaints and many thanks from the Chief Engineer. That ship had a good soul. He motioned me to continue.

"The Ottawa was and is different. It brought the best and the worst out of me." It had a Soviet soul embedded in its Hull. I tried to explain so he would understand that I was different than others without sounding certifiable. I didn't have to try hard as he was now hanging off my every word.

The smile was gone from his face and was replaced with a twisted ambience of a child seeing a treasure just within its reach. He just glared at me and said, "I didn't understand what you meant; that which comes from within?"

I looked around the confines of the room we were in and let out a sigh of relief. He had asked the right question.

"When I was a little boy on that Dive Tender, I knelt over the dead body to find his life experiences transferred to me. I was shocked and stunned at first. In years to come, I would learn to cope with that light."

I could sense his mind moving in many directions and the questions would come all night and into the next day long after the sun came up over the Bedford Basin.

"I want you to come with me and smell the morning air". We walked up a few flights of stairs and exited in full sunlight on the roof of the bunker. There was a low haze out on the Basin that morning and just below me was the empty shell of HMCS Saint Laurent. She was a destroyer, the first in her class designed by Canadians, built by Canadians and sailed by Canadians; my early years onboard a National Sea Product trawler had set the stage. The second time came after she had been mothballed here at the ammunition jetty.

I had spent a few nights in the water unnoticed by caretakers swimming her full length, touching the barnacled sides of her hull below the waterline. Once, I felt her move as if a heart beating but had been warned off by what I thought was a Commissioner slowly walking her top decks.

"You see that ship below us?" I nodded and he said: "this will be your future if you stay in the Canadian Services. You don't belong here and where you come from gives you an unusual edge." It was my turn to ask the question.

We were both standing next to each other when I felt the first strange feeling of energy. I turned and said, "She won't make it to the wrecker's yard, nor will I." He didn't say a word.

I left the facility exhausted and without any confirmation of my intended future as it pertained to my immediate environment. I had overnight duty and the woman I lived with would not suspect what I had been contemplating over the last twenty-four hours. Bev had warned me about this relationship, but I did not heed her words. I had this thing about her finding me, not I in reverse.

Transportation was waiting for me at the gates where a Commissioner was calculating his watch rounds for the day. I opened the door of the Van and slid into the bench seat behind the driver. Maybe I had said too much, or maybe it was just not enough. This I did know, I had to get some sleep.

I arrived at the Windsor Park Married Quarters, where another vehicle was waiting outside of the quarters. It was a large a black car with Department of National Defense plates on it.

A driver in uniform got out of this vehicle and motioned me to him. "Seaman Trenholm, please come with me."

He opened the back door for me and I was motioned to get in. I was the only occupant other than him sporting a totem pole on his beret. This was a Military Police Driver. The drive was familiar as we pulled through the gates at CFB Shearwater coming to a stop at one of the hangars.

"This way, please."

I stepped outside of the vehicle and was led into the hangar where a small jet was at rest. I thought I had stepped into the crap this time. There was no one to answer that question, but I was sure there were going to be many questions at the end of this journey. So far, everything seemed friendly.

I walked up the gangway into the cabin of the aircraft to be greeted by a familiar face from the past. "Hello Frank, it has been a long time."

There are light surprises, dark surprises and "Oh my God" surprises none of which could describe the look on my face or the feelings within.

"Not long enough" I retorted with a past sense of humiliation at the hands of this Bermuda resident.

Here sat a man who had tested my own understanding of reality. During a winter naval exercise onboard HMCS Ottawa; we undertook a paint ship routine at St. Georges on the small island of Bermuda. It was a brief respite from the somewhat harsh winter of Fishery Patrols in the North Atlantic. This was undertaken by the Canadian Navy to monitor and inspect all vessels within the 200 mile sovereign offshore zone of Canada.

Bermuda offered the luxury of warm days, immaculate beaches and entertaining night life for a sailor like me. We would never wear uniforms ashore so as not to distract from the local population. It is better to blend than have to defend one's nationality when on foreign soil.

We arrived at Bermuda early morning and I was stationed at the starboard boiler punching fires. This was a term used to describe the manual lighting of fires within chambers to heat the boiler. The Ottawa was a Steam driven Frigate (or destroyer) with duel boilers and twin turbines as a propulsion method. Like all the Saint Laurent Class Frigates, she was slow to warm up, slow to cool down and very touchy with incorrect handling. I would learn that first hand standing in front of the boiler.

There were multiple chambers which incorporated the components to generate steam for the turbines. Each chamber was numbered and color coded to correspond with the Water Tender at the Main Console in the Boiler Room. From here, steam was transferred to the Engine Room where huge turbines would convert steam to shaft revolutions and speed. One stoker, one boiler and several chambers to monitor according to the lighted board on each side of the boiler console. A Petty Officer and a Master Seaman would sit side by side monitoring many gauges and water levels. When the need for engine revolutions were called from the Bridge, a light would be switched on from the console and myself like many others before me would engage a chamber to heat the boiler.

Each chamber had a set of flaps for air, a sliding nozzle for fuel and a fuel valve to be turned on and off according to the boiler's needs. During normal steaming, the boilers operated in a steady manner of one or two chambers, but when in maneuvers, the need for speed was required at a moment's notice.

The Ottawa had just made its entry into St. George's harbor and I was fortunate enough to be on duty alone at the starboard boiler. Lights were flashing and I was manning each chamber in perfect rhythm. Nozzle in, flaps in and locked, moving the lever for fuel in the downward position.

One and two lights were lit, then three and four would come on, then five and just as fast, the color lights would extinguish themselves. Fuel shut off, flaps unlocked, retracted and finally the nozzle tube would be pulled back a foot or more depending on the adjustment. Anything less than fast was unacceptable, but even worse was the error of a flameout when the boiler lost its capacity to generate heat.

I learned a valuable lesson that day when I extinguished all the fires because I saw all the lights go out on the console. I screwed up or so it seemed, but I knew it was the water tender that had turned off all the lights. Whether it was in error or intentional, the responsibility rested solely on my shoulders. For a brief moment, I looked over at the Master Seaman behind the Console and saw what I had suspected.

Now there were two ways to approach a flameout and the correct way was to use the manual igniter attached to the number 1 chamber. It required cranking a rotary feed handle which would ignite a low flame on the nozzle and the procedure was to reinsert the nozzle, flap and fuel immediately. I knew I was going to be blamed.

Upon entering and leaving harbor, there would be hell to pay from the Engineering Officer during the expected investigation. I chose the alternate method taught to me from a stoker who had served onboard one of the Tribal Class Destroyers from World War Two.

Within an instant of shutting down the boiler, I reignited it by pushing in the air flaps of #2 chamber and turning on the fuel valve. The nozzle assembly was drawn in by the air induction of the flaps so that the oil from the nozzle ignited straight off the back wall of the hot boiler.

All the lights were back on and all chambers were back in operation. No one was wiser except for me and the man at the console for different reasons. I learned from that day on, to do what I was told, but never to do it without exercising my own judgment.

I was not cut out for blind obedience without first assuming the consequences of my actions, no matter who was in charge. It's a lonely way of life when you alone decide that course of action.

The Engineering Officer was not amused and rather than have to believe an Ordinary Seaman over a Master Seamen, he took the intelligent route and had all the oil bunker tanks tested for water; this might explain why the flameout was caused by anything other than human factor.

The Engineering Officer was competent, intelligent and very much a professional individual. I learned another valuable lesson that day from what he did not say. Meanwhile, watch routines were established while in port and the remaining off duty personnel were allowed to go ashore to experience the Island hospitality.

He and I, (another Marine Engine Mechanic) changed out of uniform and into civilian clothes. We hit the bars along the Cruise Line's Pier. I assumed that where there are luxury ships, there would be luxury ladies. Unfortunately, he was not a drinker and even less than a ladies man having grown up in Montreal as English speaking. He was cautious to the point of not taking chances in places where he had no knowledge. I on the other hand was inclined to see this as a non-hostile environment in need of island culture participation.

We went through a few beers, a few bars and a few conversations with some very nice girls on vacation. I intended to stay whereas Mueller decided to go back to the Ottawa. He tried to get me to leave with him, but it was to be my destiny to remain alone.

I was feeling the lightning bouncing off my spine, therefore as usual, something was about to happen. After a few drinks, I began to feel very strange with a long legged blonde who had showed up at the bar as soon as Mueller had left.

I don't remember much after that until I came to sitting on a chair with a fan slowly revolving over my head. The lights were dim, my elbows were restrained to my side and there was a man looking into my eyes from a seated position.

"How do you feel?" said the voice with a somewhat blurred face.

It took me a few moments to realize my situation and another few moments to rationalize that this had been totally unexpected.

"I'd feel better if my hands were untied and I was free to return to my ship." That was all I could say.

He leaned over and pulled my ear until my head was twisted exposing the other side of my face. I could see another man dressed in shorts and a colorful shirt sitting on a table with one leg lifted off the floor. The face was familiar but there was no recollection.

"The restraints are to keep you from hurting yourself. When a person comes out of a dream, they sometimes react violently" said the man sitting to my left.

Little did I know that I would need such a thing!

"You can release the restraints now", spoke the voice with command and authority. I relaxed more with his words rather than the actions of the individual releasing my arms to my lap.

"You do not remember me, do you?"

I reached deep into my memory for a minute or so and responded:

"I think I've seen you in my home town of Pugwash at the Cyrus Eaton Compound a long time ago." A smile broke across his face as he looked down at the floor.

"You've had some damage done to you over the years ago but it won't be permanent." I had no idea what he was talking about.

"You will remember many things, but this will not be one of them for a long time."

My mind flashed back to Newfoundland and wondered how much this man really knew about me. It was a long time ago, yet he knew more than the Navy which made me suspicious of this mystery at hand.

No one knew for sure what was going on in my head at sixteen years old. I would not be the one to disclose that I was having visions over and over again; most of which I chose to forget for the better words of survival. He glared for a few moments and spoke to the other man still standing in front of me with a cold but respectful stare. He never took his eyes from mine.

"Take this young man down to the garden and leave him with the usual."

That was the last thing I saw, a lightning strike. When I came too, I was standing at the door of a stranger who was kind enough to call the police and have me picked up for something I was sure I was running from at the time.

The Bermuda police were kind, respectful and prepared to give me the benefit of the doubt for my behavior. I was released and caught a cab back to the ship just before daylight. I was slightly confused and without much memory other than having one too many drinks with a good looking woman. I never stepped off the ship again except for garbage disposal.

The next morning, I was called to the brow and was handed an official package addressed to me at the brow.

The note read, "Keep this gift as a token of our future friendship. Do not discard it and keep it in a safe place." That's all it said.

I took it below and opened it in the privacy of the boiler room. I didn't understand at first, but I had enough sense to place it in an empty five gallon can of hydraulic fluid. I placed some machine parts into it to replicate the weight of oil and replaced the cover securely back on the bucket. I then returned it back to inventory and would not retrieve it until Halifax. By then, I had hoped to figure out what was going on.

Pugwash was haunting me again as I lay in my rack or bed (as it is called) that morning. We were heading for an exercise with American vessels. I began to think then dream of Pugwash when a voice brought me back from recollecting that memory and an even greater mystery.

"How have you been since our last meeting?" The interior of the plane's cabin was beautiful as he motioned me to set down in a plush leather chair.

"Would you like a drink?" I remembered the last time I awoke to have a conversation with this man. It had been facilitated by a drink.

"No thank-you" I said, "I am on duty and need to get back to the base."

A smile broke out on the aging face of this elderly man before me.

"You don't trust me, do you Franklin or do you prefer Frank? May I call you that or do you just prefer Trenholm?"

I decided to clear the air here and now.

"Sir, and I apologize if you are not one, but what is going on here?"

He took a sip from his drink and gently placed it on the table. He had such a kind face but the two gentlemen sitting across from each other were not so likeable from my vantage point. He was aware of my uneasiness and motioned with a slight head movement and the other two guests quietly removed themselves.

"Franklin, I want you to feel comfortable and consider me a friend. We have more in common than you realize and I am going to keep you alive."

Now, I was silent and hanging off his every word.

"It seems you have made an impression on a few gentlemen, none of whom I would trust in any given situation. They seem to believe you have something that might be of interest to them. I know for a fact that you have and with the right training and friends, you may well surprise yourself." He smiled again. "It will be no surprise to me. Did your father ever mention anything that the divers may have recovered from that old U-boat wreck?"

My mind was in reverse gear now. I had never said a thing to this man about the wreck. Then it dawned on me. This man had been talking to the other gentleman from the bunker or I had been given a truth serum back in Bermuda. He must have sensed that I was double checking our previous conversations in thought and gave me no chance to build distrust towards him.

"I knew your father from Pugwash as well as Shepard Trenholm, the harbor pilot. Our paths crossed a few times in the shipping business. Mr. Eaton's Import and Export business was quite extensive."

I wasn't falling for that variation of this and that which had to do with that and this, therefore we all knew what was going on.

"As far as I know, Dad was a lobster fisherman. The only wrecks I remember were of him pulling my brother Gary out of the truck after he fell asleep at the wheel."

He was studying me now and I was studying him. It would be easier if I could remember the circumstance of his visits to the Eaton Compound in Pugwash. I would have to go back so I could move forward with trust or distrust.

"Franklin. Franklin!" I could hear the voice but it took me a few moments to come out of the daydream.

"Did you read the book I left for you back in Bermuda?"

My mind had just started to engage this conversation while the thoughts of Bermuda were still fresh in my brain. This time, I tried to stare right through him but it was difficult. The aging face that seemed so kind and gentle was trying to manipulate my emotions.

"I did, but I wish I hadn't."

There, I finally said it: "Why me?"

It took what seemed longer than it was as he slowly raised himself from his comfortable chair. His words were exact and the impact was directed solely at me.

"Do you believe that you have a destiny?" I thought for a moment and shook my head at first then I smiled to myself. Yes, I did have a destiny, but this was not to be what I had envisioned.

"Yes, I believe I do have a destiny, one that I am trying to fit into with a volunteer program."

He smiled and gave me a second glance with the smile gone.

"I sense you do not trust me and I may have given you a good reason for that."

I was tired, over stimulated and just sitting on the edge of my seat. I wanted to get up and leave, but I also wanted to see where he was leading this conversation.

"Listen," I said. "If you knew so much about me, why for what reason would you give me a book on the Royal Canadian Mounted Police? There are two Constables that live next door to my mother. I've had so many run-ins with the RCMP over the years I have to believe that the further away I am from them, the better."

I didn't mention about the incident after I had returned from Bermuda on that ill famous trip. I had a vehicle drive right up behind me and drove me off the road doing fifty miles an hour. I ended up over the hill in someone's kitchen with me at the steering wheel of my car. I was not going to think about it right now. It was eerie to say the least and more like a story that would fit the Bermuda Triangle rather than Dartmouth.

"How many uncles do you have?"

This was a very strange subject but maybe it was more to relax me or it was asked to distract.

"I have three Uncles on my Father's side and three Uncles on my Mother's side."

I went through the names: Herb, Chester & Sheldon in that order. Then there was Garret, Okie & Opie. Three were in Canada and the other three were in Holland. It was into the Thinker pose; once again, my mind was in reverse.

My mother was a Dutch war bride and my father had been a Canadian Soldier in the Royal Canadian

Electrical & Mechanical Branch during World War 2. Dad never spoke to me about the war years as if they were memories that were valued as private.

There were some pictures of him that I once found in a drawer around the house but my mother scooped them up and put them away. I guess they were not to be played with by a little boy.

"That is not entirely correct," he said with a full blown grin on his face. "You have another uncle on your mother's side. I presume that your father never shared that with you before he died."

I did not wait to inform him that he was wrong, but I was kind in how I related fact.

"If there was another uncle, I would have known about it. There are no pictures of him with my Dutch grandparents nor has anyone discussed it."

I remembered back to the time I had spent in Holland after dad passed away and there was nothing to base his information on. I just shrugged my shoulders and said: "I'm not aware of that."

"Your uncle's name was Frits Vanderheide. His death certificate stated that he died as a result of kidney disease, but the building with the records was destroyed after the war."

I guess I needed to have a chat with mom the next time I saw her.

Before I had a chance to digest what I'd just been told, he added: "Your uncle had blonde hair and blue eyes."

There, I was finally realizing what his objective had been. The subject was back at the U-Boat and I knew exactly what he was trying to tell me. He also knew by the look on my face exactly what I was thinking.

"Sir, I really need to get back to my base. I haven't slept in a few days and I am on watch this evening."

I really wasn't but I needed to get out of there and in a hurry with my own secrets intact. I stopped for one brief moment and said; "I do have more uncles, one was in the Mafia in Boston and the other one was a Submariner during the War."

They came every summer during lobster season to visit as I was growing up. There was a lot more to figure out, but I would be doing that on my own in my own time.

"Franklin, I will be in touch again once you get settled into your new career." There was a smile, a wink and a click of the heels. "Remember what I told you, trust your instincts and be careful what you wish for. I have a sense that your wishes will probably come true."

That was that. I stood up not knowing whether to salute, click my heels or just lower my head and exit. I chose the latter and said good-bye. The driver and vehicle were waiting for me aft of the airplane. I couldn't understand what the whole point of this exercise was or maybe there was no significance in at all.

Maybe it was just a distraction to see how I would react. The guy was British alright. He was German too and what he wanted, he would never find.

The drive back to Windsor Park was uneventful. The driver never spoke nor did I. As we pulled up in front of the married quarters, I said thank-you and headed to my apartment on the first floor. I could hear Amber sniffing behind the door as I unlocked it and was greeted by a sixty pound yellow Labrador retriever, wet tongue and all. I hooked the leash on her collar and out into the backyard the two of us went, oblivious to this day's events.

This was a good place so what was nagging me from the back of my mind? I had a woman who disliked me, a young son and man's best friend. It was absolutely perfect and the dislike was perfect for not giving her an advantage.

I went to sleep restless waking up several times in cold sweats. Something was pulling me into time and no matter how much I tried to concentrate on other things, I kept ending back in Pugwash. If uncle Frits were still alive, who had he been? Did I meet him at some time or was he just a figment of an old man's imagination.

The next morning came and I was off to work. I drove a Vega with a head gasket problem which was one of General Motors not so successful line of vehicles. As I would accelerate, smoke would rise from the exhaust pipe. I never had the money to repair it or the heart to get rid of that car.

My other shipmates would know my whereabouts travelling across the McDonald Bridge, so the nickname, "smoke on the water" stuck. Traffic was stop and go from Windsor Park to the Dockyard and the puffs of smoke coming from the Vega were part of that routine. I heard a soft voice in the back of my head saying; "Don't make smoke if you want to get out."

The drive across the bridge that morning was uneventful except for the daydreaming of former days. I had been here before, yes, ten years ago travelling over this same spot on the way to visit my father at the Camp Hill hospital. What an unusual joke had been played by my family for uprooting me from that tiny fishing village on the Northumberland Strait.

A smile came across my face as I looked into the rear view mirror. It is a difficult thing to escape one's past especially if everything reminds you of past events. That said, I had a lot to learn about the future and from my past the best lessons had already been taught.

Halifax was where my father finally died having suffered months of cobalt radiation to eradicate the brain tumor which in the end took his life. Camp Hill was the Veteran's Hospital. On the occasions I would come to visit, I could not remain in the hospital for hours either in the waiting room or the ward where he spent most of his days. Mom was kind and would give me the latitude to cross the street and walk among the grave stones alone.

I parked the car in the overflow lot just outside of the dockyard and proceeded to the gates where the Commissioners were quietly checking personal identification cards and passes. I was dressed in uniform and knew most of these guys by sight or from the many drinking establishments. Commissioners came from the ranks after retirement which allowed for needed income or that personal attachment that came from having a job you really enjoyed or loved. Sometimes it is difficult to let go of the military connection.

I was passed through the gate where the many jetties were filled with ships of the Fleet. There was one though, gray and black tied up to a newer research vessel called the Quest. The name on the other vessel was the Sackville, an aging research vessel itself. It carried the name from where I had been born.

Just then, a warm gust of wind filled my mouth and nostrils with the telltale smell of diesel oil. It reminded me of summers past and there was no mistaking the secret which existed between us as I headed across the docks to the Submarine Squadron's buildings.

The Sackville was a Canadian Navy Auxiliary Vessel and when not tied up alongside the Dockyard was occasionally out to sea on research. I had spent a couple of weeks onboard her somewhere between the Bedford Institute of Oceanography and the Royal Canadian Navy. I was soon to discover that I had spent a full day onboard her as a very young lad in Pugwash Harbor.

Dad would say that "boats are like old girl friends; they either bring a smile to your face or a sinking feeling you need to let go of." How right he was and this one had put a smile on my face. Throughout the sixties and the seventies, Sackville's history was kept under wraps until it was decided that she be restored to her original configuration as a Flower Class Corvette.

I had been born in Sackville, New Brunswick and though our connection could have ended there, we were bound together in more than that. The last time I had seen her in the Dockyard, its hull was black and gray and most of her War time gear had been removed.

Years after I had left Halifax, on May 4th 1985, HMCS Sackville was officially given its due recognition. I assumed the Premier of Nova Scotia had initiated this, but I was wrong.

Fully restored with a home on the Halifax Waterfront during the summer months and a winter home back in the Navy Dockyard, HMCS Sackville was finally honored in her own rite. Who would have known? Of course, I would be the last to understand. I was gone from Halifax and without the important parts of my memory, it would be a while. Maybe that was the plan all the time.

I was looking at the past and into the future at the same time. There was no mistaking what I was now feeling. It was September 1968, September 1979, September 1990 and September 2001 all co-existing at the same time. I felt cold, sick and unable to stand at that very moment. I didn't belong here anymore. I felt as if I had reached the point of no return.

What was so important about September that it kept nudging me from behind as if to say; "Remember me?" It seemed there was an event every 11 years that would stand out and nudge me to stop and think.

There is a purpose to all things whether we like it or not; I was learning that the future was always in control. Yes, the lessons of the past always made for easy transitions, but they never showed a fellow everything. I can only assume that September carried with it the start of every season of education that I had lived throughout my life. As time would pass, I would learn the years following the month were in error and implied nothing as to what lay ahead.

8

The Echo Within

The walk across the dockyard facilities was always a pleasurable experience taking in the many views of daily naval activity. Civilians and military personnel all working hand in hand yet separate in their own identity. This was the way of the world I lived in now.

I made my way around the Syncro Lift where vessels were lifted out of the water to be worked on by Dockyard workers. Alongside the Submarine Squadron Buildings, three O-Class Submarines lay berthed side by side; there was no activity on any of the hulls. A large blue building stood before me now with its metal sides and roof. This was the Submarine Squadron and the place to which I had been called to report for class-room study. Upon entering the class-room, I saw before me the same Officer who I had met years before in the National Sea Products Office after the incident on the Cape Hood. The insignias on his uniform had changed but not the facial features. I wondered if he would recognize me.

I was in for a surprise because not only had he recognized me, he was the one who had summoned me here through the intricate operations of a "Need to Know basis." Sometimes, it is not a good thing to want to know everything.

"Please take a seat and relax; this will be informal."
He motioned another officer to sit with us who I once
remembered having tested him for the physical endurance
test at CFS Shelburne.

I had been an Assistant Physical Education &
Recreational Instructor and tested some of the Enlisted
Men & Officers around the remote Bases of the Navy. I
had transferred back to the Marine Engineer 312
classification several months ago and found myself on the
other side of the table once again. It was just like old
times.

"How've you been, seaman?" He said without a
smile.

I could see his lips moving but my thoughts were
back to that night on the George's Banks where a
crewman had lost his arm.

"I'm fine sir; it's been quite a while since we've
talked like this."

The other Officer was looking at me and then back
to the Admiral wondering what was truly in play here.

"Yes, it has. I meant to check up with you after that
incident on the Trawler, but it seems you left the area to
fish lobsters back in Pugwash where you grew up. How
was it? Did you find what you were looking for?"

I had to do a double take here, one to recover what I just heard and the other to think what was coming next. He saw the look on my face.

"Sir, it was nice to get back to the place where I grew up."

He smiled and said; "How is your wife and child doing? I believe she was pregnant with your first back then."

He had me by what he already knew and was just letting me know. This would prevent me from telling an untruth should he ask me a question on anything. I would rather tell the truth than get caught up in a lie to a Superior Officer.

"She's fine sir, at least the last time I heard from her. She is now out in Alberta hoping to practice law someday. I'm single and trying to remain solo, if that can be done."

He just smiled. "Good, I love a happy ending."

Without skipping a beat, he began discussing my future as it applied to a new direction for me.

"Oh, by the way Seaman, I meant to ask you if you found what you were looking for in the old 851 Trade."

It was my turn to not skip a beat.

"No Sir, Trade 851 sure was challenging, but I made my way through it without getting caught up in the internal stuff. I did sustain an injury getting over an obstacle, but I recovered fairly well."

I am sure the other Officer felt we were discussing the Physical Education 851 Trade but I knew the Admiral was implying something completely different. It finally dawned on me how I came to be offered a position back in my hometown so soon after the Trawler Incident. Someone had wanted me out of the area, especially the spotlight.

"I am glad to hear that. It's not too often we lose a man from the Engineer's 312 Trade to a land slot and get him back, especially if he has any talent."

He looked over at the other Officer and casually said; "This is the crewman who placed a recovery line on that fishing gear before his vessel lost it at sea a few years ago in a storm. The one we recovered with that rare species of whale entangled in it."

He was now directing his gaze to me.

"The Scientific Community gained a lot of details on what we were able to recover because of your quick thinking that night." My mind was in fast rewind now and what I remember most of all was the fact that no one had been impressed back then, least of all this gentleman.

"Sir, what kind of a whale was it?" I had an interest in all marine life which would explain why I chose to work for the Bedford Institute of Oceanography a few years back. I was truly interested in what he had to say.

He smiled; "it was a species that we have never been able to study up close let alone recover its carcass in such good shape. Unfortunate though, it was decided not to disclose such a rare find."

He was now busy sorting out some papers in front of him on the desk. I was starting to get the drift of what he was implying after having spent many hours watching the towed sonar arrays from the stern of the Destroyers I had served aboard.

"I've looked through your records and do not see diver training or any attempt to take a course. That is very odd because I was informed that you were a fairly good diver in your early years."

I felt his stare on my forehead as I raised my head. He's informed, well informed and what could I say? I guess what was said at the Ammo Dump did not stay in the Ammo Dump.

"Yes sir, I learned to dive from a couple of old Clearance Divers when I was a young fellow back in Pugwash where I grew up. They kind of taught me the ropes and a few other things." This was the safest way to explain my training.

"Interesting, I was to understand that you've done some salvage work as well. I assume those old divers taught you well without any documented training." It was his turn to think out loud.

"How would you like to do a special course in underwater submarine inspection right here at the squadron? The Ojibwa is slated for lift out next week so you could see what these things look like out of the water. I'm sure it is not the first time you've entertained a concept like this. Why not make it official?"

I couldn't believe what was happening here. On the other hand, I am sure he already knew about our little secret back home in the waters of the Northumberland but not its whereabouts. I believe I may have not been alone when I went back to Pugwash that time after the Trawler Incident. In fact, the real reason might just be why I was asked here in the first place.

"You can stretch your legs if you wish; take a look at some pictures of submarines on my desk. You might be interested in some that are pretty old while the others are quite interesting to say the least."

I took his advice, got up from where I was sitting and glanced at several photos from the table. It was the photo of two World War 2 Submarines which caught my attention; U 190 & U 889. They looked very familiar to me. I noticed I was being studied very intently and my choices were of interest to the Admiral. I carefully switched my train of thought and picked up a photo of another submarine which was completely out of the water. I turned and asked what it was.

"That is an Echo 2 of the Soviet Fleet. It is rare that we could get one of these photos, especially with such close-up views of its hull and interiors."

I laid the photo down and picked up the German U-boat ones and asked if they were still being used.

"No, these are photos of surrendered German U-boats at the end of the war. They were both IXC/40 class style boats. They did a lot of damage to our shipping in the beginning, but we gave it back to them near the end. The guys in these boats were the lucky ones."

The next three hours were spent in areas that escape me now, yet brought a warm feeling of endearment to all the photos I had a chance to look at and to forget.

This was the start of my launching point from the Navy compliments of any and all training that I would need for the future; my future. In less than one year, I would be in the place they call the Echoes or as we called it; Lake Echo 1 & 2.

Little did I realize then, that Lake Echo would be the death of me; yet become a new beginning. There were forces at work here that even I could not identify until it was just too late. Call it Karma or any other natural event, but I had achieved a balance between guilt & innocence and paid for it with my own life.

Not all things are explainable, anymore that they are attainable, but here I was with everything I ever wanted placed right in my lap. I wondered what the good forces of the future had in store for me now. Had they told me then, I would never have left the security of the Canadian Military.

Finally though, my past caught up with me handing a surprise that I would not quite remember for years to come. Of course, it did start out as a little needling in the greater sense of the word which would either end up telling one big truth or a whole bunch of lies.

That's how it began. It was January 17th of 1983 that I found myself being brought to the hospital in an ambulance by the same people who had compromised me through sheer ignorance. But it did provide for the basis of a new life without having to operate so remotely ever again.

I knew I was going to die and I knew who, when, where and from that vision alone, I was able to change the outcome. I would survive because I had made it too easy. The day before all of this had happened; I had called the Poison Control Center asking them for information on a container that had been left in my garage. I was told that it had the components of Sodium Pentesol in it and was primarily used to euthanize animals. My telephone lines were not secure and I had known that; I had planted the seed.

I waited for the shadows to come out from the woods that morning which they did. Had I not made that call to the Poison Control Center the day before, I would have been found hanging from the rafters in the garage.

I went to sleep with the sound of laughter in the background with a needle stuck in my arm as a reminder that men of Preston never forget. But as luck would have it, January 17th was my Aunt Catherine's birthday and somewhere between the time my heart stopped and my inner vision took over; I realized that I did have another Uncle who was now encompassing every part of my being. It was my Uncle Louie, Catherine's husband, long dead but somehow had come to life in my death dreams.

I found myself sitting at a table at the age of 5 or 6 with Uncle Louie sitting across from me with a bottle of beer in front of him. His eyes seemed ghostly, but either as a dream or a vision, I saw a shot glass with Cape Cod on it filled with a small portion of beer. Some things are best kept to yourself, but what was translated between this Uncle and I seemed to energize my brain's functions. I started coming out of it slowly at first with double vision and saw all the reasons why I had to leave Canada; soon.

It was Ralph Waldo Emerson's Poems that came to mind just before I came to and went off to sleep for what was supposed to be forever; "Do not go where the path may lead, go instead where there is no path and leave a trail."

I had crossed into no-man's land where things were not always what they seemed. What I had been doing was not sanctioned; therefore, I had become expendable. Uncle Louie had lit the Torch for me in a world that had been filled with darkness for those brief few moments.

This day was January 18th, 1983.

9

The Devil's Staircase

September of 90'

I along with several others had made our way back from the Middle East onboard an unscheduled Military flight near the end of September in 1990. They are most often referred to as Black Operations.

I had left a wife and two children behind a week earlier. On that morning, I had dressed myself in green sweat pants, white sweater and running shoes. It was not my occasion to talk much in the morning nor had I dressed in such careful attire in years. The others needed to know my situation.

I felt compromised and I needed others to get the message without a word spoken. I had dressed as a PERI 851; "Physical Education Recreational Instructor 851" without a beret on my head. The important part would be understood. This would clearly illustrate in discreet terms that I had lost my cover because of my past. My cover was best described as a beret; one that was required in the Military as an alternative dress. I was also the Keeper of all U-851 artifacts.

A PERI 851 has a sole objective to keep the troops physically fit and emotionally strong in times of peace until they are needed on the battlefield, natural disasters and or peacekeeping. I knew what was behind me and what lay in my path as an obstacle.

On the night of 1-2 August of 1990, Iraq invaded Kuwait. The UN Security Council was in full session and we as a personal family were climbing the Devil's Staircase or in simpler terms; driving up the Eastern Seaboard in a Ryder Moving Van with a 1979 Buick Regal in tow. The Buick was not a new car of sorts, but a reminder of the old days when the Director of CIA would make his daily trips in and out of Langley with something in the trunk. It was an endearment I had allowed myself as a reminder that simplicity was foremost a convenience and Casey was no longer at bat.

The Canadian Defense Department were contemplating a Task Force to be sent into the Persian Gulf in the form of 3 ships, two of which I had served on. By the time August 9th arrived and the Canadian Navy had been authorized to participate, the perfect screen fell into place for me. I would enter as a Canadian, act like an American and leave most likely as a Frenchman with none the wiser.

I had been researching Iran Contra debacle to assist in sorting out the facts in the correct perspective. The Arbitration Court of the International Court of Justice was still collecting particulars with field interests throughout the globe. If the United States and Iran were now working through some back channels of participation; how would the Arbitration Justices initiate a determination with an undetermined influence of The Courts responsibility? The goal was to gently lay aside the mystery and high lite those involved. But like all things, nothing was so simple; I had a wife and kids who needed to be safe in case I never returned.

I had another issue that needed dealing with and that was the method I would need to get my wife and children back into the safety of close family support. I had been walking on some very unholy ground the last couple of years. Iran Contra was rumored to have been just a screen to transfer nuclear technology for oil rights. Who knew! Somewhere between Kuwait City & Dubai, the truth might just present itself or forever slip beneath the sand.

Upon arriving in Hingham, the Canadian Task Force had sailed from Halifax on August 24th with Athabaskan, Protecteur and Terre Nova. A week earlier, I had deposited the contents of the Moving Van into a storage unit just outside of Naval Air Station Weymouth. My two other team members were already on Base, out of sight and for now out of mind.

By now, the Canadian Task Force was alongside in Augusta, Italy and had been brought up to speed on the menacing Exocets that they might have to engage once the ships entered the theatre of operations. A few of us could not forget the episode of the USS Stark in 1987 nor would I forget the next few days.

Waiting for a go ahead on any Operation can be vexing, but we had been juggling so many others, there was no time to even catch my breath. There were many places that documents had been left in secure locations and I probably added a few thousand miles travelling between Bourne, Hyannis and Newport, RI. And of course, I was also under surveillance so being doubly aware was most important.

PERI in Persian Mythology are the Fallen Angels. I was not officially one of them, but had been adopted for other reasons. This screen would serve as an alternate plan to be extracted if my cover had been blown. I was on notice it had.

Over the years, I had been privy to many conversations from behind the scenes in which everyone had to be friends. It was never easy to say the least and in most cases, the endeavors were fairly complex. I had one contact who had retired from the Government as the Attorney General and another that I would see in Washington DC when passing through the District.

By now, things were beginning to heat up a bit in Hingham and Taunton as National Guard Units were called up along with Reserves and Regular Forces. I really didn't know what Saddam Hussein had been up to, but over the course of several years, I learned a lot didn't make any sense when it came to his actions. Such was the case of the USS Stark and several events that followed which included me down in Tampa, Florida. I would never make the same mistake but came very close to doing it again on September 11th at the Portland Airport.

The Director once said that Saddam was like a cobra, "You never know who is holding his attention or teasing him with a stick." There would always be an Egyptian Air Force Officer in one ear and CIA in the other giving him conflicting information and advice. He wasn't that very smart even though he professed the knowledge that he had been a lawyer back in Egypt during the expulsion days. I always felt he was to be pitied rather than praised.

I awoke the next morning, slowly dressed and opened the door to see if my son was still asleep. I knew it would be sometime before I saw him again. I picked up the little guy still dressed in his pajamas and gently hugged him with a kiss on his cheek. At five years old with blonde hair and blue eyes, this little guy was my pride and joy. He was a Trenholm through and through with a touch of Italian that was embedded in his character as well as it was embedded in my own now.

"What if I did not return; how would he ever learn the truth?" I would make sure I would return. As I came out of the room and downstairs, I walked over to where my wife was holding our baby girl and gently kissed her on the forehead. There was nothing that I could say as she transferred the baby over to my arms. I'm not sure if it's the talcum powder or pampers that give babies their unique smell, but it is a smell that stays with you in memory no matter the events.

I kissed her cheek and forehead before I gently placed her back in her Mother's arms. I nodded and casually glanced back to say; "see you this evening."

It took a few moments to get myself out the door and down the front steps. I needed to loosen up the muscles and joints before this morning's run. I was careful to stretch out the muscles in my legs first, arched my back and limbered up the best I could before the jog I was about to take.

I was taking in my surroundings to pick up on the things that were now watching me from other driveways. I smiled as I leaned forward to touch my toes with the palm of my hands. "Today is going to be one of those days for reflection," I whispered to the ground.

I started with a slow jog at first until I reached the top of the hill on Canterbury Street. Nothing of interest caught my attention until I reached the driveway opposite of the Tower Day Camp. A stand-in motioned me into the driveway where he casually took my place and I headed down the lane where a car was waiting with the side door open.

My stand-in would have his hands full as he finished the jog down to the car that had been parked at the Auto Hospital on Rockland Street. It should have been another couple of weeks before I would have heard his story, but I had returned with no memory. His training was more intense than mine which had been on evasion tactics so I'm sure he had fun while I was gone. Everyone, who had come into contact with me, realized that I knew no one; and maybe that was the plan after all.

I slid into the back seat of a vehicle with tinted windows and pulled the door closed. The woman sitting in front on the passenger side handed me a blanket to cover myself; to supposedly take a nap. The drive was silent as we turned out of the driveway to our right heading back the way I had just come. There is something about a drive with a blanket over you passing by the place where the last seven years of your life are a woman & two children you love very deeply. The thoughts become pure and everything suddenly becomes very clear. I had a job to do and from here it would begin. So how does one get from Hingham to Kuwait City without anyone knowing about it? The launching point would be the Naval Air Station in Weymouth. As we made our turn onto route 128, there was no mistaking a three car line up parked off to the side of the street waiting to enter the surveillance game with me as the subject. The gal in the front seat spoke without turning her head; "we are so sorry you got burned here, but if there is any conciliation in all this, all things will be made right when you get back.

My stand-in had long ago reached the car at the end of the street and had returned the Ford Taurus Wagon back to its owner on Deep Run Rd; a street that was nothing more than a dead end. Jack was gone, but his aging wife would not recognize the slight difference in our height, our eyes and voices as her car was returned and my own vehicle removed from her garage.

A helicopter was already in prep mode by the time I reached South Weymouth. The drive through the gates had been uneventful with my old uniform on and the new identification beyond reproach. At the hangar, there was only the whine of the helicopter blades as I made for the hangar.

I looked at my two buddies waiting for me in front of a pair of big doors and shook my head. "You guys aren't going to believe what I just had to do to get here?"

The voice following close behind me now said; "And you aren't going to believe where you have to go."

I felt the blast from the rotors at about the same time I felt the chills radiate down my spine. Nothing surprised me anymore. The Recovery was on. Actually, it was more than that. It had been long rumored that Kuwait held the key which would unlock the Iran Contra door of horrors but it had only been a rumor. No one in Kuwait would be opening any door for an investigation coming from the ICJ, but Saddam had changed all that; it was his greed for the ultimate weapon, something that would not hold him back from using if it was to be his decision.

My relationship was not with Saddam, but I did have a connection with a Company called Space Research

Corporation. It was owned by an ex-Canadian who could open doors at the drop of his hat; this one he opened for us.

The nice part about being Canadian is that no one takes you seriously and you have few enemies around the world. You can pretty well travel anywhere you want and that always gave me an edge without a target stuck on my back; that seemed to have changed most recently.

The flight out of Weymouth to Otis Air force Base took us directly over the Sheraton Tara, Braintree in a wide arc. I had reason to look fondly on the structures below as that was the place I had met my wife. It seemed like yesterday as I remembered the Hotel the way it was in 1983. The sound of the rotors above was taking me back to the first time I had arrived.

It was the morning of December 23, 1983 when I left Dover, MA for the last time; my Aunt Etta giving me a ride to the Bus Terminal in Braintree. I said thank-you, good-bye and got out of the car very quietly. I turned and said my final word.

"Tell Grace I won't forget. And Dad was right about Uncle Howard." I could hear her scratchy voice from behind asking for a better explanation; I had none. I just knew.

One Saturday, I brought my cousin into the Commonwealth Pier for a day to visit some Canadian Naval Ships which were in Port for the week-end. I needed some private time so I left him in the lounge in the capable hands of stokers. I'm not sure what they told him about me, but he had a new found respect with a hidden fear of my presence. I couldn't blame him for that. We spent several hours onboard the Preserver and left with three sailors in tow. The rest is in the Navy history books of how 3 Canadian Sailors ended up in a club called "Sanctuary" which was nothing more than a Night Club outside of the City, but to me, it was subliminal. There were to be more secrets in the future for that town.

There was no doubting my arrival in Braintree at the Sheraton Tara, where a room had been reserved in my name for the evening. I had caught a cab from the Logan Express Terminal to the Tara soon after my Aunt had dropped me off. Upon entering the Tara, I was greeted by two suits of medieval armor standing alone on either side of the main entrance with two smiling faces behind the guest reservation counter. I approached the desk and gave my name to the staff with the reference that a room had been reserved.

"Welcome to the Tara, sir; your registration has been taken care of. Let me escort you to your room;" He said it at the same time I was about to produce my identification.

I said, "Thank you, it's so nice of you to take care of such things."

With that, he smiled and said; "Mr. Smith works in mysterious ways" and handed me the key to the room.

I opened the door to a pair of Queen Beds overlooking the Highway. The room had been prepared in the ancient style with all the necessities of privacy. There was not a hint of technology within the room.

I spent the next couple of hours going through the material that had been left for me to digest. It would be a slow descent to the most southern point of the country before I would fully understand what had been expected of me to accomplish within a month. The timing was critical because of the winter routines that had been established by friendly assets. I never take anything for granted and trust only the research that I or another of my group had completed. Because none of this had been our research, it was time to free the mind. There were rumors that an unknown branch of the Sicilian Mafia had been discovered operating within the United States. I only had a few pieces of information that the Attorney General had resigned to take up a place in California to follow through with an investigation that he had begun through connections in New Hampshire. The Admiral suggested that I was the man for the job, but as always, there would be no easy beginning.

The swimming pool on the lower floor would be a great place to relax and come up with a plan that would ensure my return if I was successful or had gotten lost along the way. The Sheraton Tara would serve as that anchor. The water was warm; the pool was empty except for the gentleman who placed a closed sign on the pool door after I had entered. His only comment was that I had 30 minutes to enjoy the pool alone. It was more than enough time. I finished up my water time just as Maintenance returned to unlock the door for other guest use.

As I was returning to my room, I began to sense a presence somewhere in the building which had me puzzled at first. This was a female entity with barely audible thoughts, but thoughts never the less. It had been a long time since I felt a female presence who could think outside of herself. A vision of Frank & Theresa had come to mind with a telltale exposure that Kenneth (surely not my father) had not been configured into this time.

I had come from Musquodoboit Harbor just months before with the vague memory that I no longer had any alliance to the IMP; (just another entity into which mystery was its second nature.)

After showering and resting on the bed while I read some material, I felt an inner need to socialize down at the local pub called the "Naughty Knight."

There were a few patrons at tables sitting around an open fireplace while at the bar, sat a few ladies discussing work and friendships. In this setting, I could not help overhearing all the conversations that were being held throughout the room. It was the two girls at the end of the bar that were beginning to hold my attention before I realized that what I had felt after leaving the pool was now sitting directly in my eye sight. I would need to be on my best behavior if I were to go through with what had formed in my mind. I would need a place to become invisible in should this next operation go bad; if it was for Justice, then it would not.

This endeavor seemed more like a basket game as this would be a Full Court press if nothing else; a term used to designate that all hands would be on deck for a run against a very experienced defensive team. If we failed, then our only memory would be that of the USS Maine. I also had to consider that someone would be sitting on the sidelines with a foot out trying to trip me up. Trudeau would be sitting the picket up on the way in and the Admiral on the way out. These were the considerations I had to consider.

They say truth is stranger than fiction under severe circumstances but here I was looking at two ladies; one a blonde and the other a brunette.

"Oh how the past & future intermesh all at the same time in mysterious ways," I whispered to myself before I stood up and walked to the other end of the bar where they were sitting.

I motioned for the bartender to treat both ladies with a complimentary drink and returned to my seat waiting for the acceptable response. It came with a smile from both who turned to look my way with some amusing humor as they returned to talking with each other.

Before leaving my room, I had stood in front of the full length mirror looking at a 28 year old man. My hair was dyed black; the beard was gone with only a small mustache in its place. Wearing black pants, shirt and boots, I looked like the average Spanish priest but that was not the look I needed right now. I added a light tan corduroy blazer with a Tiger Eye gold ring on my wedding finger; one that my Aunt Etta had given me in 1969. How times had changed?

The blonde would look over my way every once in a while until finally I got up from where I was sitting and moved over to their place at the bar. The other girl was the first to say thank-you for the drinks. I responded with a "you are welcome." I introduced myself as Franklin and they in turn said their names.

She asked me what I was drinking so I motioned to the bartender and asked what my drink was called to which he replied; "It's called a slow comfortable screw."

I nearly fell over backwards with the comment but before I could turn red in the face, she responded "cute."

There was an awkward moment until the blonde asked if that was like "sex on the beach."

The bartender was quick to respond with all the ingredients and before you knew it, I was invited to sit with them. It was a fun evening until the bartender motioned me with a heads up look. I casually took in my surroundings around the room spotting the newest arrival. The northern group had arrived which encouraged me to leave as well. I stayed just long enough to escort the ladies out to their vehicle where I asked the blonde for her telephone number. She was surprised I had asked for it by the look on her face.

She said let me get a pen to which I said, "no need, let me take a guess at it. If it's right, you will go out to dinner with me the next time I am in town, ok?

"Deal," she said. Little did she know that I had this thing for people in the banking industry?

"Okay," I said; "the first number is 7. My birthday is the 4th and my father's was the 9th. That's 749."

There was a look of amazement in her eyes.

I looked deep into her eyes and said; "the next number is 2 which stands' for you and me. Your friend is alone which means she is just 1 and the last two numbers must be the same as the first number. You came here first which made you the first number 7 and you are leaving here with someone you might like to spend your life with. That makes me a number 7 as well. So the number is 749-2177."

Her mind was racing now and before she could say yes to what I had just said, her response was; "What's the area code?"

I took the time to look at the other girl with her and politely said; "Seeing you are with a Kennedy, I can only assume that a Kennedy began his term in 61 as the big guy which also makes him a 7. The area code would have to be 617."

A smile cracked across my face. "No need to write it down, I'll remember that."

That was the end of the beginning as I opened the passenger door for her. She never took her eyes off of me as they backed out of the parking lot. I returned to my room only to find another file folder on my bed. It had been labeled. Another hour passed before I finally drifted off to sleep.

The next morning was spent putting all my gear in the right order separating the file folders that would be left at the front desk when I checked out. The other ones were to be dropped off in Philadelphia. The driver and car were waiting as I walked past the knightly armor with a smile on my face. I would be back someday.

After what seemed to be a short drive into Boston, the driver dropped me off at the South Station where I bought a one way ticket to Miami via Philadelphia. It was an uneventful descent except for spending Christmas Eve in the same place where the Declaration of Independence had been signed.

There was a rebirth that night for me as I stood outside of the Terminal and pondered what all of this had meant. I had wanted to be free and my wish had been granted; if only I could keep it. I ended up at the Southern tip of the United States.

I arrived in Key West on Boxing Day where I spent my first day being a tourist taking in the Truman Annex, the Naval Base and of course Dirty Harrys', a local watering hole for all Navy types. If you couldn't find your Ship's Crest hanging on Harry's wall, you just weren't navy; it looked like the whole Fleet was in town.

My time in Key West was basically short except for some extra effort spent Para-gliding behind a Cigarette or what the natives called a gunge-runner. I couldn't see what lay 90 miles to my east but I could sense what I was about to do.

I was coming as a thief in the night and for reasons I could not possibly fully understand, it had to be done this way. I spent some days in the local Hostel amongst the many Nationalities while on other days; I would be sharing the time with the Navy types. The only recognizable feature that would even separate me with the others was the gold Tiger Eye ring. Like me, it had been stretched to the limit to fit on every occasion, no matter the endeavor.

The day we were readying to cross over to the other side, the Big Guy showed up to say hello. There were a hundred other ways we could have done this, but for some reason, he felt this would be the one operation that would make up for every other failure they had endured over the years.

On the way down to the docks, I could not help remembering what I was now looking at. It had been in Roosevelt Roads years earlier sitting dormant while we were in a paint ship's routine onboard HMCS Preserver. I spent an evening on the Bridge drinking Budweiser and sharing stories with an American watch keeper in January of 1980. Yes, I had been here before.

They say if Nova Scotia was the front door to Cuba, then Key West was the back door unless you chose to walk through mine fields or swim through some nasty barriers from Guantanamo. I believe now the guy upstairs wanted to send a message that only one person could ever possibly understand whereas the Admiral wanted to make his one creation have some infinite meaning he would take to his grave.

Now the Chief, he had another reason but it was long after I had recovered my own memory before I finally understood his objective. The best way to get outsiders to be insiders was through the Military Service. This operation would explain it or kill us all. I did not enjoy the thought of the latter, but I had seen myself return to the

Sheraton Tara in a future image, so I had nothing to lose except my freedom.

We boarded the Hydrofoil with the Admiral grinning ear to ear. Though there were no markings on the side of the vessel, the brass plate in the wheelhouse left me with no doubt.

The sun was setting as we were leaving yet there was no mistaking the throngs of people along the inner harbor. From the stern, we could all see behind us the many delights of human behavior entertaining the people with their acts on the waterfront. No one would have noticed anything else but that activity this evening.

Just out of sight of the land, the foils which had been pulled up tight to the hull were lowered into the water. What had been a low rumble below our feet turned into the sound of thunder vibrating up through our legs.

The water was calm with no obstacles ahead on our projected track; the only thing touching the surface was the glare of our teeth. No one outside of me knew what we were looking for. Until I could walk amongst the people; I had no idea what we were getting into. It was rumored that the package would move every few days to a different location which most likely was the route of lovers, here one night and then in another place but always coming back to the same place after a few weeks. The Chief described it as pure intelligence wrapped up like fast food, we called it McDonalds and the name stuck.

We were up on foils for about an hour when the sleek silhouette of a helicopter passed over maintaining the position just ahead while a second one was taking station just beyond our stern. We were in the cradle now waiting for the next 30 minutes to pass ever so quickly. The choppers were cloaking us while high overhead something else was jamming everything between us and the Island. We were running in the dark and had been briefed that when the boat started its turn to starboard in a wide arc, that would be our cue to debark the ark. One man at the helm and another below with the turbine; would confuse the Coast Guard with our intent. No lights, no warning; it would be done in two's with the last man going in alone.

The Hydro-foil started to lift on our portside at the beginning of the turn and with the count of thirty seconds, all nine of us slid off the stern on the fly in the correct order we had rehearsed with no gear other than our clothes tightly sealed around our bodies. These we would need after making shore. There were no guns and the only tool we all agreed to take was our knives. How could we open beer without them?

Within the Harbor of Havana, there were three foreign guests that would provide the perfect screen; A Soviet submarine tucked in behind two Destroyers. We would blend in, do no harm, leave that invisible message and disappear forever allowing the professionals to do what professionals do and the amateurs to go home.

Satellite photos would have a different description of that evening in the future, but the language would be the same with the Sub & two Destroyers now taking on a human appearance. The language of linguistics always amazed me when converted to print.

Cyrus Eaton had been here many times along with his son and grandson to walk amongst these Island people without being bothered by Cuba's Military organization or Secret Services. We would follow in the same footsteps.

The moment we began hitting the water in pairs, the two choppers above kept on going in on a straight line with lights on; simulating what I suspected was a simple game to test the Island security. It was described in simple form that they would fly in for another 3 nautical miles making outbound turns each going the opposite way. It was the hook formation to catch attention and then draw anything that may be looking our way away from us. It had worked and three hours later we swam ashore unnoticed at the edge of a mangrove peninsula.

Could all of this have been done from the helicopters instead? Sure, but Fidel would have known. It was explained to me that there were eyes at every Military facility known who would report the quantity of occupants on every aircraft departing the Island Chains.

On the other hand, the Hydrofoils were never considered for anything other than drug interdiction and were they to leave Key West outbound; the Coast Guard would only suspect a sunset pleasure cruise. No, Mom was the word on this one and there would be no leaks.

I would like to say that we were inserted into this hostile land dressed in all the gear that would warrant a special operations infiltration unit, but I can't. When we emerged from the mangrove area onto an unpaved road, what the natives saw were nine happily toasted Russian sailors all dressed in naval uniforms; we looked the part.

Currency is the universal language when it comes to socializing while beer and vodka can open any door without knowing the native languages. Singing the one song we had been taught actually made us invisible.

The Island of Cuba was ours to tour with the ladies in tow. We offended no one, never got too drunk and made our way from one end of the Island to the other enjoying all the delights of its people and good people they were.

There were many nationalities represented in Cuba but what surprised me the most were the amount of French Canadians who were in residence here. I had memories of the FLQ incident back in Canada and this being the place where the kidnappers had found sanctuary, but I never suspected such an open door policy. But the focus was on finding Castro's love nests which had been mostly identified by assets as possibilities to what we were looking for. We had two days before the Soviets sailed and then our invisibility would completely disappear.

My job was to find the interpreter who processed his thoughts in English; it was the same as looking for a needle in a hay stack. I remembered that analogy never really sat too well with me after Lake Echo, but that was how it felt. It wasn't until we accidently blocked a Cuban jeep because some of the boys were trying to do a Cossack dance in the middle of the street.

Our Spanish was poor to say the least while their Russian was even worse. In that moment, a Gentleman sitting in the rear seat stood up speaking to us in perfect Russian yet his thought processes were in perfect English. I slipped back behind one of my comrades very quietly as I realized that I knew the man now standing. I was being a bit over cautious, yet the chances he would recognize played heavy on my thoughts. The highest rating in our group picked up on my nod and made his way to the side of the Jeep explaining that we had been at sea too long and the sun here had made us very thirsty.

He apologized and shouted for us to move and straighten up which we did grabbing hold of a comrade who had fallen down right in front of the jeep.

"You can take the Cossack out of Mother Russia, but you can't take the dance out of the Cossack," I said with a grin from the shadows. I saluted while the gentleman sat back down on his seat and motioned the driver to move on. The rear lights disappeared at the next intersection beyond a hotel heading out of town.

"Trenholm, we need some transportation" demanded a voice from behind me. I realized that I had never stolen a vehicle in my life so why start now? But this was not the time to think about the law; we were way beyond that now. I liberated two vehicles that had been parked to the side of a make-shift entertainment facility. It had probably been erected in the last few days because it had not been on any of the surveillance photos from Montreal.

The range of the device that had been placed under the bumper of the jeep when our buddy fell only had a mile frequency in which we could track it. Fortunately, speed is not important to Cuban soldiers. The one part of my amnesia which I never recovered was the events that unfolded from that moment until we were leaving in a local's old fishing skiff from the backside of the Island. Someday, should I ever return, I will bring Fidel's personal flag back to him in the spirit of courtesy. We had caused no harm, there was no alarm and what we recovered would solve the mystery that had perplexed a few over the years.

Three Cigarette Boats were waiting for us and like those naughty drug runners everyone had heard so much about, we had blind approval to leave the Cuban Coast and stealth approval to enter the Bahamas who welcomed us with open arms. We made a few stops along the way in different Keys for each of us to disappear. I had wanted to see Mrs. Eaton who now resided in the spectacular delights of the Florida sun before I made my way back to Key West, so what better timing.

Anne was a gracious host and as much as I wanted to stay, I knew I had to go. She had heard word that Henry Simmonds was looking for me in the Keys now and I assured her there would be no mistaking that I was not unaware of this. "I have something which I brought with me from Pugwash and I would like to leave it here when I return in a few days," I said with a smile. "It will bring you no harm and you are probably the only person I can trust right now."

Anne was an astounding lady, an honorary "still being" of the 5th Republic. It was the one secret we shared and one she honored without reservation. She had done a lot of good over the years in her own way.

I left for Key West the next morning on a Shrimp Boat out of Marathon that had been in for repairs. There was no mistaking that smell of shrimp as I sat on its stern making 8 knots with the decks bathed in bright sun. We arrived as the sun was setting pretty much the same way I had left, but this time I was alone or so I thought. I got off at the docks and made my way over to Dirty Harry's to see if any of the others had made it back. The place was full and making my way over to the bar was not an easy endeavor to say the least. Liz was tending bar and when she saw me, there was a hoot and whistle coming from her that could silence a room.

"Where have you been, you were at the Hostel and then you were gone. Nobody knew where you went." It was the Australian upbringing that made her so caring towards others and I had been included.

We chatted while she served her patrons without missing any requests. She was a little heavy set, but had a face of an angel; she could drink me under the table as I once learned at Hemingway's bar a couple of weeks ago.

"You haven't seen the red head around since I left," I asked.

She paused for a moment, then said; "He disappeared the next day after you, why?"

"No reason," I said, but I did have a reason. I will call him bald for no other reason than his hair, but he was the eyes and ears in Key West. He knew who was coming in and who was leaving. He had an unusual knack to know when somebody was friendly and when they were not. He was good on the ground but what was most important, I could trust him even if he was with the Federal government.

"Listen" I said, "I'm going up to Miami in a few days. If you see Red, just say I was looking for him."

"Frank, stay out of Miami, one of the boys came through there a day or so ago and the Cubans were on the warpath. I don't know any more than that, but I wouldn't go."

That was Liz, always in touch with the natives.

"Well then, maybe I will stay for a while. Know of anyone looking for some extra help?"

"Yes, I do. There's a Spa down on Duvall Street. They're looking for a night person to manage the front desk." She saw the look in my eyes and said; "relax, they're harmless but they do need someone and its nights so you can have the days on the beach. It might be a good learning experience for your future."

With that information, I went down and applied. I was hired on the spot and for a week, it was great. The problem with the winter in Key West according to the natives was that Snowbirds come from every province, mostly good and a few bad looking to get some product home. I would run into some people I knew which I knew was not good.

The Haitians and the Cubans were coming down the highway looking for faces, certain faces and I had a feeling that I was one. My concern for the Snowbirds was not of my fear, but more so that they not get drawn into something that had no connection with. It was time for me to leave.

I made Ann's place that evening and stayed long enough to drop something in safekeeping should I ever return. I said good bye and headed up the coast to Cousin's Pearl or at least that is what I called her. Maine in the winter is much more relaxed if you have another place in Florida; which they did.

I arrived in Clearwater that evening just in time for dinner but no one was there; they had not come down from Yarmouth, Maine yet. I could go to a hotel but maybe I needed to call in first. I used a pay phone on the street to call Montreal. That evening, I was heading North on a Greyhound Bus.

I arrived in Boston on a Sunday morning. The ride was uneventful except for the many stops along the way to catch up with the flow of information from Miami. Someone in the Coast Guard had been leaking information but there was no one to pin it on. We would remain unknown. Never the less, it had no bearing on us because what the Cubans were looking for; had to do with some missing Libyan stuff. It is always better to be safe rather than sorry. I had to call a new friend.

The pay phone was at the end of the lobby with very few people in the terminal. I put in a Quarter and dialed the number, the one that the Blonde had given me at the Sheraton Tara exactly one month ago. It was now January 20th, 1984.

A woman's voice answered the phone. "Hello."

"Hello, would Teri be there please," I said hoping for a "yes, she is."

"Just one moment please, can I ask whose calling?" There was a pause from this female voice to which I answered, "Its Frank." I could hear a few low voices in the background asking who was on the phone.

"Hello." It was a childlike voice that answered the phone.

I said, "Teri, it's Frank; we had drinks together at the Sheraton Tara just before Christmas."

There was a pause; then I realized my mistake. I corrected myself and responded; "It's Franklin, I apologize about not adding the lin, but it's what I use when I'm working."

"Well hello, where are you?" I told her that I had just arrived in from New York on the Bus and was heading to the Cape for some relaxation. "I just wanted to call and say hello." Half an hour later, she showed up in a white Cutlass, Oldsmobile with a rose on the face of a license plate on the front bumper. The thought of a Prime Minister passed through my mind for his careful wearing of a rose in his lapel during public forums.

She proceeded to get out of the car and said; "Why don't you put your luggage in the trunk." We spent a wonderful day together.

At the end of the day, she dropped me at the Plymouth Brocton Bus Stop just outside of Hingham. She was a good soul for sure. The bus arrived right on schedule and we said our good-byes. I promised that I would call the next evening which I did.

Aunt Cathy was very surprised to see me. I knocked on the front door and entered. She was on the front porch having a Vodka and orange juice.

I just shrugged my shoulders and said; "Got a room?" It was as if I had never left. I had completed what my Aunt's husband had not. Uncle Louie had been a good guy caught up in bad timing and too many loose lips.

The chemo treatments that my Aunt had been taking were on hold for the last several weeks so she could regain her strength. Theresa would come down on the week-ends; pick me up when I was available. On other times, I would stay in contact by phone. She was unique in her own way.

In March, I felt it was time to go back to Nova Scotia and bring a final close to my life. The Admiral and Chief thought it was a bad idea under the circumstances, but I needed to bring it to an end and recover that which I had left behind.

I drove from Hingham, Mass. to Amherst, Nova Scotia in one day. I spent that first night with my Cumberland County Representative discussing most everything except business. He brought me up to speed on the Cargill Inquiry. It was odd to think that my uncle and I were taken out by the same instrument; mine just being a little more personal. Bob was a little surprised to see that I was still alive. He encouraged me to return back to the States as soon as I could but I first needed to bring him up to speed.

"Bob, my father always liked you and what I am going to tell you will make you think that what they have said about me is true; it is not. Brian Mulroney is going to become the Prime Minister and you will be taking McKinnon's old job as Minister of Defense. You will have the Razors' to contend with so be careful."

Poor old Bob's jaw nearly hit the floor. He said; "Crick said something happened to you last year that changed your life, I thought it was the covert stuff he had been talking about."

"Bob, I just gave you the good news, the rest is up to you." I opened the door and left.

The car was still running with my future still sitting on the passenger side. I shouldn't have brought her but it was too late to turn back now.

I went to Port Elgin first, Pugwash second and then onto Halifax. It was dark as we pulled up to the entrance of Citadel Hill where I made the last phone call. The true conversation will never be repeated, but I left there knowing what was ahead of me and what I was about to do.

I got back in the car, looked at Teri and said; "We have to leave and we have to do it now. I wish I could tell you more, but I can't."

It took a little while, but we reached the United States Border Area just after day light where Customs and Inspection had been waiting for our arrival. At the moment we stopped for Inspection, I got out of the car while she slid over to the driver's side. I looked around and saw that no one had been surprised with my exiting the vehicle and get into the passenger side; I had driven all night. Tired and stiff, I knew I had returned back to some semblance of sanity.

A Gentleman who I remembered as just a Captain was standing beside the inspection area. Another individual who I did not recognize was sitting in a car beside him now. Maybe he was the new Commander.

We were waved on after a respectful; "Welcome."

I told her to stop the car. I rolled down the window and the gentleman standing next to him, held out his hand. I handed him the papers. I said, "As we agreed?"

He smiled; "We wouldn't have it any other way."

A few miles from the border, we both could hear the sound of a helicopter fly directly over us on its way to some unknown destination and with that, I fell asleep. I slept until we pulled over several hours later. I tried to rationalize what had transpired since I had been gone from

Nova Scotia. It was something that was entirely out of my control, but at least I was free.

We booked into a country hotel which came with a water bed and Jacuzzi so I knew I could finally relax.

My first call was to Edmonton Alberta while I sat in a bathtub of cold water to clear my senses. I knew Bev would be searching my mind as well as I would be searching hers.

She answered the phone and I said, "It's me, is the divorce final?"

There was a pause after her first hello so I knew that she knew there was something else between us on the line.

"Yes, two months ago" and there was just a click as the line went dead.

There was nothing more to say as I replaced the phone on the floor. The horn sounded, I was free as I let my back, shoulders and head slip beneath the water; all in that order.

"Hey, wake up! I swear you could sleep anywhere." I opened my eyes to see the face of my buddy with the sound of the rotors almost sending me back to sleep.

"Gees, you are a piece of work," he said to me and with that, I started to focus on the job ahead. Yes, the job ahead, but would I remember it? The future had turned invisible which caught up with what I had left behind. This was how I could always see my way back.

10

A Mind Lost

September 1990 "again"

The first moment I opened my eyes, there was nothing to see or very little to hear. There was a movement of water somewhere below me, ever so gently lapping upon some hidden object. I waited for my eyes to adjust to the darkness which had enveloped my senses. There was no light. I listened in earnest for sound or a recognizing factor that would somehow orientate me to these unknown surroundings; there was none.

The air was damp and cool with a heavy musty smell. My head was hurting, my body was aching and I was trying to push the thoughts of blindness from my mind. I was in a semi-prone position on a lumpy but otherwise comfortable material covered with a soft fabric, silky to my touch. When I tried to move, a stabbing pain shot across my ribcage, my head began to spin and the taste of salt water ran down the back of my throat. I passed out.

I came to and rolled over on my left side coming to rest on what felt like wood. This action sent my mind into a panic. My next thought was now questioning where I might be, a coffin! There was a feeling that I had been here before. My arms flailed and my feet kicked at the invisible box I had placed myself in, but the touch of silk became the lining I remember my father laying in at his funeral. I was not dead yet, but there was this unmistakable feeling that I was close. With only air above me, the silky fabric at my feet, a wave of panic settled into a very uneasy feeling. I was not on the bottom of the ocean.

"Where am I?" I whispered into the dark.

There was just the sound of lapping water beneath me.

"Where am I?" I repeated. "Someone, anyone, please answer me!"

The first cognitive thought that made any sense came moments later when I realized I had no idea or memory of anything about myself. But wait, the image of my father had been real, or was it? "What is my name?" I thought. "Hey! Where the hell am I?" I hollered!

Looking back now and knowing more about trauma, I can appreciate how remarkable the human brain is when working properly. I also know what the mind can do to any person when confronted with situations that cannot be understood or defined. I had been trained to know when to shut down and or move forward.

The loss of senses and the absence of knowledge is a frightful experience. It can send an individual into a hysterical event of fear and panic. The worst was yet to come for me and slipping back into a state of unconsciousness, I was spared the situation only to be pushed into a state of terror and dreams. Falling through the air and landing hard became a repetitive nightmare, to wake in pain as I landed on some hard formidable object.

I began fading into alien images, some of sounds, faces and strange machines hovering over the water. There were voices and yes, my own voice! There were lights all around as my mind finally began to grasp something vaguely familiar. It was the heavy sound of engines drowning out my thoughts. I could see the flight suit of an Air Force Officer, (odd I thought, this wasn't their recovery) leaning towards me through the flames. His words would haunt for years. "Do you have something for me?" It was just thoughts.

I was falling again, fully expecting the impact; I prepared for the pain. I thought death was better than this so I waited for it to end, but it did not come. The nightmare reversed and I was sent back to the place of safety. Once again, I was flying above it all. I couldn't grasp the fact that I was not in control of my own fate and kept returning to a different point in time; that would change.

Training dictates to observe every environment, no matter how friendly before entering, to establish the entry and exit points. We were still flying over the Atlantic and in a few hours would be east of Provincetown on Cape Cod. If you enter without an exit strategy, chances are your stay will be permanent. It was my desire to return home to a family who truly had no idea what I had been up to. I had left in such a hurry under a veil of secrecy that few would have understood.

Instead of a high altitude drop, the plan was for something simple. There would be no static line; just a gentle free fall. It works best at the point of no return. You just simply exit from the belly of the aircraft.

I stood up from the jump seat and moved forward up to the cockpit station. Once again, a three seat formation of pilot, co-pilot and engineer sat before me as I put on the headset dangling from the bulkhead. Everything was coming and going in threes this trip. I tapped the engineer on the shoulder. "Gentlemen, I have a special water taxi inbound to those coordinates we discussed before takeoff and I would be honored if you could get me there on time."

No one spoke as the chalk board came up from the right side of the pilot's seat. The pilot turned around with a half sheepish grin and stated the obvious: "There are a lot of what if's down there and if you miss your ride or they don't show up, we cannot retrieve you and your guys."

I looked at the badge of his flight suit which identified him. "You won't have to," I said; the two triangles were now folded into each other.

It was my turn to sport the full sheepish grin. "You guys ever hear of the Psalms?" Sometimes, just a nod and a thumbs up is all one needs to ease the tension.

Respect comes in many forms and I understood their concern for my welfare. There were not going to be any screw ups in the return as there was leaving the States several days ago. There was not going to be that easy drop off on the tarmac at SOWEY either - "NAS South Weymouth."

I should have known then that I was trying to convince myself because I knew otherwise deep in my gut. Back-up plans had been made the day I had left 76 Canterbury with the two of us going different ways. Leaving my vehicle at the Assinippi Industrial park, the other thought this the perfect analogy as I disappeared into the woods off Canterbury Street.

The Engineer turned and spoke: "Just wanted to let you know that we are three hours out."

I passed the word along to the other guys and started making final preparations with the two packages fastened securely on the deck. I had reached my point of no return. There was no going back! It was not so much that I was needed in Canada; it was that I was wanted here more or at least that is what I wanted to believe. The future would prove that I was right.

"Psalms 73 boys, I just hope it's still there."

It was two hours later that the Crew Chief ordered the ramp down and out we sauntered into the darkness of the night. With two close friends I never really knew nor did I want to in public, the one finger salute was all that was needed.

The September air was clean and cool throughout the drop. The water was just a little uninviting at first, but only for the first moments. It was somewhat foggy below from above, but as soon as we splashed, the stars were all ablaze. I hollered over to where the other two had come down and asked the question; "Are you guys okay?" There was the usual "F-yes and this bites" coming from out of the darkness. Everybody who finds themselves in this situation relaxes by joking and we were no different.

I could hear it before I saw it coming from out of the west. It was the unmistakable sound of a Navy Seasprite's rotor blades still quite far away. Over on my right and out of the darkness I heard; "Did anyone check their horoscope today?" It was the sound of the departing Hercules above that smothered out the sound of the approaching helicopter. With the blinking of lights, a life raft landed within our hap hazard circle. The three of us thanked our lucky stars that night and the presence of the raft would make for an easy recovery. I stayed in the water as the others climbed in and were recovered one by one. The first two of our little group were winched up without a problem and while waiting for my turn, I visually located the plugs and the burn kit to send the raft to its watery grave.

I heard before I saw the Chopper dip its nose and depart ever so slowly to the east. I had a bad feeling about this one but out from the north came another Helicopter, this one quieter and just skimming the surface. The lights came on as it hovered above.

Like clockwork, the recovery harness was being lowered to the water's surface. I had pulled my chute in the standard carry bag and slung the harness under my arms. I really did not like surprises and even less, a change on the fly.

Being the last of the three to be recovered from the life raft, I decided not to sink it and motioned thumbs up. I had opted out of taking one with us because of my own faith in the higher power to be on time. This one would be spared.

For a brief moment, I thought there was a smell of shrimp in the air. I realized that my drop off point had been changed without my knowledge. It was the wrong time of year for Maine shrimp in the water of the Massachusetts Bay. It was A-typical.

The Seasprite was the workhorse of Weymouth Naval Air Station. Those old birds had long outlived their effectiveness in the new era, but were perfect for a low keyed operation off the coast of New England. It was routine. On the other hand, the Canadian Sea Kings were not in much better shape either. The Gulf War would confirm that. As I was being winched up into the chopper's side door, the configuration of what I was looking into was far from a Seasprite. The newer version of a Seahawk unfolded before me. Things were not only feeling bad, I started to sense my own death. That is not a good feeling to have when you are not sure who is on the other end of the recovery line.

I slipped the recovery bridle from beneath my arms and looked carefully throughout the craft.

"Remember the entry and exit points!" I whispered to myself.

The sound of the pilot speaking over the com did not escape my sensitive ear, nor did the sinking feeling in my chest. The particles within the night air were beginning to charge with electrical activity and the tingling along my spine sent my eyes searching for the exit door. The Pilot turned and looked at my face.

"Ghost Ops One, this is Osprey." There was silence for a few moments and then other monotone sounds, "Alpha One is onboard, eta, 23 minutes." Crawling to the jump seat, I briefly reflected on the night's jump from an unmarked C-130 cargo plane.

From the corner of my eye, I noticed the flight suit of a United States Air Force Officer, (odd I thought, this wasn't their recovery) leaning towards me aft of a dimly lit cockpit. A voice was trying to speak to me over the noise of the Helicopter's engine; "Do you have something for me?"

I stood up, slightly bent over and realized that I had been lifted into a trap. It was an image that neither left me with comfort nor fear. I remembered the plugs had not yet been pulled on the raft before being lifted into the belly of the helicopter. It was still below me somewhere.

There are never any survivors in Operations like these when the past facing you has it in their head you just don't exist. It was at this time in thought that I sensed rather than saw the streak of light heading towards the very craft I was now standing in. Out the exit I threw myself just in time before the sky lit up with a devastating explosion.

It is not the drop that kills you, but rather the sudden stop which follows. Noticeably, there was sufficient water beneath me as I landed on my back. Both legs were curled above my body allowing the dry suit I was wearing to absorb some of the impact. The pain cannot be described in words and for a brief moment, I remembered a few days before when two buddies and I were cascading across the Kuwaiti landscape. Not a thing had gone wrong but here I was alone in the water somewhere in the Massachusetts's Bay, maybe?

The human mind is a complicated mechanism at the best of times but at the worst, it can generate itself into uncontrollable fear. I was trying to concentrate on a voice from out of the past. I had been spared a tragic end but right now, the pain held the same measure as death. I caught a glimpse of what was left of the Seahawk burning off in the distance. There had been no chance for survivors to escape that wreckage let alone the blast.

As darkness replaced the glow of burning debris, what remained, slipped beneath the waves. There were no other sounds. I floated on my back for hours once I untangled myself from lines and tried to conceive if anyone would be sending a rescue or back-up helicopter, but there was only darkness.

Operations between Canadian and American entities as a Foreign Para were never an easy ritual in the open let alone in the dark. Up till now, it had been a workable situation. Canada, France and the United States were now part of the United Nation's Coalition that was carefully being put together to counter the instability in the Persian Gulf. It would not be easy in the future with smitten Nations who had their own agendas, at least for a while.

The humor in it took a few years to understand, two decades before I could laugh about it. In the end, it was not about forgiving, forgetting or the fostering of new feelings towards others. It was about finding my true self and sometimes that was not easy. Like a hermit crab that leaves one shell for another, chances are that some other creature has already taken up residence in it. I learned to leave a little surprise just in case I wanted back in. That was pretty impressive once I regained my complete memory. The past was important.

I started coming out of the dream with the pain reminding me that this was very real. I was lost. No! I wasn't lost anymore; I was back where I grew up; just sitting in the Cemetery at the beginning of the bridge into the Village of Pugwash, Nova Scotia.

There was so much pain that my mind just tripped back to where I grew up; I had come to terms with the fact that I was dying or already dead. The view from the Pugwash Cemetery is one of a protected harbor that resembles a person's passageway from their mouth into their stomach along a very intricate route. But how did I get here? But, it was not Pugwash that I could see now; it was the Naval Observatory. How far back into time did I fall this time?

Wasn't the Admiral buried somewhere around here? I had no connection to draw any conclusion from other than the fact that I was in a safe place. It had been provided for me to recover from this last ordeal, but by whom. I could not have known this or I would have remembered.

There was a faint memory of a something long gone, a place that had provided sanctuary from the X, which now I could see flapping in the wind. It was the Flag of Nova Scotia and no recognition would ever find me here. Still, there was the sound of water lapping beneath, yet the smell around me began to take on a friendly aroma. The smell of Washington DC filled my senses as I quietly removed the wedding band from my finger. I would be dreaming solo for a long time to come until I would finally put it back on just before the final exodus.

11

The Path to Everywhere

September 1990, "actual"

We arrived at Otis only to exit the chopper and climb onboard a Belgium flagged Aircraft. The black, yellow and red color of the tail emblem was of a Nationality that I was vaguely familiar with from over the years. The interior was plush and fitted out with every conceivable option courtesy of NATO, I presumed. As soon as we boarded the aircraft, it was already in pre-flight status. Someone was in a hurry, I thought.

The next few days were a whirl wind tour to say the least. I was finally glad to be making it back to the United States via Cyprus. It was a very long flight until the unthinkable happened to which I found myself off the coast of Massachusetts with no memory, no identification, with nowhere to go even if I could have. Everything had been changed. I came to at the water's edge only to feel the strong arms of two men lifting me by my arms and carrying me to a shelter not far away. I was left there, but I was safe.

I awoke in total darkness, cold and scared. I had to get up and move around; I didn't want to freeze to death,

not here, at least not in this place. For what careful
thoughts I had left to muster into an action were almost
gone by now. With no light to see, the fear of any
movement was now holding me a prisoner. I strained to
see, I strained to hear anything, but the only sound was
that of waves moving along a rugged coast of rock and
sand. Slowly, I was able to get to up on my feet and
realized how undressed I felt, more so with the cold which
had a good hold on me by now. I was half wearing some
kind of rubber suit from the waist down and as my hands
felt the tightness of it; I also felt the other half dangling
down to my feet. It was the cold as well as the fear that
kept me searching for a way out as I had reached a point
of uncontrolled shivers.

My hands felt along a wall of stone as high as I
could feel with doors that were bolted and braced with
steel from within. Windows with glass covered more wood
and there was a table, chairs, logs and objects which made
no sense without the help of light. I felt and followed a
wooden board that ran several feet to my left then up
another few feet and back again. This had to be a bunk
bed from which I had started my search and had more
than likely woken up in it. As I moved further along, I
carefully slid my right foot in front of me so afraid that I
would reach the drop-off and fall into the nightmare of
nothingness. Instead, I found the silk again wrapping it
tightly around my body and moved into a fetal position
upon the mattress in the bunk bed. I would close my eyes
once again.

The water beneath brought me awake as it splashed against the very floor I had just walked over. I was not sure of the time lapse between those precise moments. I was at the breaking point immersed in my own helplessness, overcome by knowing nothing let alone knowing what to do. If training is supposed to take over in times like these, then my training had never been given or had I forgotten that as well?

Over and over again, I pressed my mind for any thought of memory or experience. There was no response, just a horrible feeling of isolation and helplessness. It was at one of those moments when I had finally accepted the fact that my eyes were open and I could quite possibly be blind when I heard the beeping coming from my wrist. Somehow I had overlooked the watch that had been there the entire time. I felt for it with my right hand and moved its face to my ear. I was going to be okay; I had time. Tic, tic, tic, I wasn't alone anymore; I had time.

Sounds of seagulls' broke through the watery silence somewhere overhead. Looking up I could see shadowy slivers of light. I could see, I could see.

Now all I had to do was let my eyes adjust to the incoming light. I looked around to my left then right and just above my feet; I could see four slivers of light as if inventing the image of a box. Still in pain, I moved from where I lay and ran to that box of light. That was the last thing I saw that morning. Somehow, I had encountered another object that I had tripped over. When I came to, I was lying in a liquid pool of mucus and blood. My nose and forehead were aching as I pushed myself to my knees; I saw that the light was gone.

Disorientated, desperate and appealing for some inner strength to make things all better again, tears started down the sides of my cheeks. I folded my arms around my knees and started rocking back and forth; I had reached the lowest depth from which I was slowly giving up. The night and the darkness merged, the waves became louder and the building shook from the ocean's surf. It would be a while longer, but the slivers of light returned.

I made my way on my hands and knees to the wall where the light was hastening my touch and touch I did. Pushing my face up to the lowest crack, I could see nothing, so I felt along the entire square of light. It was then that I felt the nuts along the frame of wood outside of the light, carefully placed upon bolts of steel to keep me locked in this place. I hit it with my fist, my elbows and anything I could get my hands on, but it was solid as the door I had so graciously given up on much earlier in this ordeal. I felt as if in a maze, trapped and released into another maze making my way from this self-imagined coffin into the confines of darkness then into a room with so little hope; then finally at the threshold of no escape.

Desperation can be a cruel enemy but it can also serve as the catalyst for super human strength as I was soon to find out. The nuts as I touched them began to turn in my thumb and finger grasp, slowly at first, then each one spinning off. The panel began to slowly crack open as I spun each nut away. The wind suddenly pulled it out and away from its recessed perch. I was free for that one very brief moment until my eyes adjusted to the view. It was fog so thick that I could not see a few feet before me or below the window opening. My hands were bleeding now while the rain was washing the residue from the ledge I had been resting on. Sheets of rain was washing across the structure with such force that as it stung my face and mouth, I realized just how thirsty and hungry I had become.

It was daylight outside now. Turning around to look back within my darkened prison of sorts, I saw the silhouette of the interior of an old sailing ship. Sorting out what I thought I saw yet seeing what was before me, I explored the interior once again. I found my blanket to be a parachute long opened, torn and filthy. There was no food, no water and very little light. A duffle bag of canvas tightly wrapped with cording which I opened hoping to find some food only confused me further. Nothing made sense and even less that I could remember. There was a pair of green sweat pants, socks, sneakers, shirt and papers but no food or drink. I wasn't even sure what I was supposed to do now, even more confused of what I was not supposed to do; leave or stay? What was out there? Even more the worse; I could see but I could not see through the fog, so into another maze I now found myself. I wasn't rational anymore. The process of logical thought went out that window the same as the covering which had held it closed. At least it was warm outside. With the contents of the bag, I found a way to take my mind away from the stress and anxiety of my ordeal. I removed the rubber suit and put on what seemed to be very warm and dry clothing.

Daylight began to fade just as a dim glow of a light would appear far out to the left of my view. As the fog lessened, I could see the rocks a good fifteen feet below. Foamy, frothy water was washing over them casually as fog upon the air. The light again every four seconds moving counter clockwise through an arc of intervals in time. Suddenly, I could hear the scraping and banging sound of wood on stone. For a brief moment, fear nearly sent me back into the darkness of the building where I would be safe. Instead, I stayed at the window watching an object float out of the fog, over the rocks until it came to rest below my perch. It was a boat, very small with oars still in its holders now rubbing up against the wall below me now. I knew this had to be an illusion of the mind as I kept looking at my watch and the light as it swept in and out of the fog. I became a tormented soul frozen in time with no ability to think or act with any reason of sense or sensibility.

The wind eased throughout the night as the fog lifted for a good distance. There was nothing to see except water and the shaft of light every four seconds making its arc.

I spoke out loud which surprised me; "There will be another maze if I leave this place." There will always be others until I could not move another muscle.

Dragging the remains of the parachute to the window was an exercise in determination, but not for those reasons at this moment, but for an exercise of futility. I thought if I could crawl out the window using the lines and tethers of the parachute, I'd make my way to the little boat below. I could tie it up for when the weather would be better and I could see where to go.

I tied the chute to the bunk bed and slowly made my way down the ropes just as the lines broke or came untied. I dropped into an absolute nothingness. The pain brought me too just as fast as the pain took me under until I couldn't breathe anymore. I must have knocked the wind out of me as I landed inside the little blue dinghy realizing that it was now real; there was no way to get back up into the window. I had no place to go and in too much pain to think except to only lay under the canopy which had come down upon me as I fell below.

During the time I was unconscious, the tide must have risen, for the boat and I were now drifting through a very dense layer of fog. Daylight and darkness intermeshed much like a puzzle to a child; all the pieces of understanding were there, but I could not put them together. There were just pieces of coherence, all able to create a bigger picture but with no one to put them all together with any sense or reason. The light I could see was getting closer, the tides and currents moving me along at a pace I did not understand. The sounds of waves upon pebbles and the harsh glare of light had become my sight and sound. It seemed as I was being moved by some invisible hand to a destiny I would finally understand.

I didn't care anymore just as the waves sent me on a fast ride into a shoreline littered with debris. I had sailed beyond the structure of the beacon coming to rest on a shoreline. There were lights off into the distance and a tree lined background only a few feet from where I lay rocking in the surf.

I pulled the small boat up on the shore turning it over to form a shelter so that I could sleep. Much was lost from my memory now as daylight began to take shape over the horizon. As I opened my eyes, I saw a face looking down at me. He said, "You look like hell."

"Where am I?" I responded with mutual awareness.

"You've got yourself between a rock and a hard place. You are next to the Coast Guard Station here at Boston Light. Where the hell have you been?"

I couldn't answer that because I didn't know, but I was hoping that he could.

"Do you know who I am?" I asked.

There was a moment of silence until he brought me back from the unknown. I listened for hours as he filled me in on who I was. Next came on how we met and the way to get home; especially who was waiting for me there. The route would take me to Gallup's Island across Fort Andrew then onto World's End and finally up the Weir River to the bottom of Canterbury Street. He gave me the name of my wife, her phone number and from where to call once I made it to the end of the river. There was a horse barn with phone service just inside the door.

I didn't ask for his name and trusted him to know what had been dogging me the last time I had seen him. It was no longer funny, but that was now unimportant. I had a family to get home to, or at least I thought I did.

As the years passed, I learned many things about myself. I had to relearn my own past and the truth about myself. I had to look into the mirror at the end of each day and ask; "Is this me?" So in the years that followed, it sent me on a journey of discovery and reconciliation of my past to the present, so my future would never force me again into a maze from which I could not escape, but I was almost wrong.

It took me another two days before I finally arrived at the barn where I made the call to my wife. When she picked me up, I knew then that I had changed. I was twenty pounds lighter with a new growth of beard covering my face. I really didn't know her at all, but I played the part through a very difficult set of circumstances. I had a lot on my plate and even more were the things I no longer was aware of. The sky was the limit when it came to experiencing what I thought was my life and I took many a fall after that, but I recovered each time.

My first memory flashback came on October 29th of that year. My wife & kids decided to take in a haunted house demonstration set up at the Naval Air Station in Weymouth. It was being held in one of the empty hangars where people could walk through and be frightened by all the live scenes and ghosts. I had our little daughter in a stroller when I entered the haunted house scene. It was scary, but not so bad as to be quite frightful. I turned a corner and saw a female skeleton sitting on a chair dressed in a wedding dress. When she saw me, she stood up and held out her hands and said; "I've been waiting for your return, where have you been?"

I started having images that I had been here before and by the time I made it through the haunted house, I was not prepared for the gorilla which seemed to come out of nowhere carrying a chain saw. It started chasing Theresa with no evil intent until I stepped in the way of it. I was laughing so hard by now, more so as the wife was high tailing it across the parking lot with the baby stroller out in front of her. She was scared, but that is what haunted houses are for.

I was a bit taken back but recovered to realize that all of this had meaning, at least to the guy who gave me the free passes that night. I had a tough time trying to figure out who I could trust and whom I could not. The guy I worked for had an in-law with the FBI and a cousin flying Marine One, so the free passes were much appreciated.

The Iraq War came to a close while thousands of men began returning home. The following year, there was an Airshow held at NAS Weymouth. Once again I had free passes to take the family to see it for the day. There were aircraft from other bases which had participated in Dessert Storm and were being honored by display. There were strange sensations of closeness as well as a familiar level of having being here before. At the end of the day, a MIG Fighter came down in a rough landing when its nose gear collapsed. It was a Korean era fighter that had been restored by some enthusiast. Having a ghost tagging along always made for interesting happenings, but it was nothing I could put a face to; it was just always there.

I was writing stories now which sometimes would take me into the early morning hours. I really had a vivid imagination or at least I thought I did until the day I had an urge to write a letter to the Whitehouse. Tell me what I was thinking and I will tell you that I was just the messenger. I wasn't sure what was driving me, but I had such sympathy for the hostages that still remained in the Middle East. I am not sure why, but I felt some responsibility of a job left undone.

I confused the messenger with Einstein who had written a letter to then President Roosevelt and somehow had been trapped within my own consciousness. I knew what I was doing, whereas I had very little capacity to understand why. The formulas which were appearing on paper did not make things easier for me even though they had some meaning to which I should have shared; but did not.

12

Nobody Gets Left Behind

It was the morning of September 15th that I sat down and wrote a letter to The President of the United States. It may not have been the brightest thing to do under the circumstances, but for the last several months, I had been studying what I did not understand. Those who knew me in this period of my life had little idea that I was testing religion which almost drove my wife crazy for not eating pork. It was the one thing which had been a staple in our diet. That week and a half that I was gone a year earlier had changed me; I was tolerant of other's beliefs and even went the extra mile attending the Roman Catholic Church every Sunday. No one could say that I wasn't hunting something.

I wrote President Bush a sincere letter which probably had too many opinions in it and just a little too much imagination but I believed so much in what I was trying to do. For the life of me, this became a very common occurrence over the next few months. I am sure the Secret Service did their job quite well and figured out that I was perfectly harmless. On the other hand, the President's Chief of Staff probably felt obligated to utilize the benefits of having a letter writing campaign coming his way.

President Bush never saw any of the letters I wrote to him, but I can well imagine he knew of my whereabouts from that moment on. I encouraged the confirmation of Clarence Thomas, warned him from travelling to California and finally told him that Lincoln was a dead man while Saddam had been misunderstood. Looking back now, I can see the reason why we had been created.

1991 was the culmination of a very difficult time in my life. I was operating from a higher power without knowing why but as things would have it; this era of hostages was coming to an end.

There were 5 numbers that stuck in my head and no matter how hard I tried to figure out their meaning, I would end up more confused. It was 45545. The nice part about not knowing everything is that you can make a mistake here and there without wrecking your confidence. There were some highs and there were some lows, but in the end, I was a much better person for what I had been through.

Christmas of 1991 was a special time for me when I finally found out that one of the Hostages; Higgins I believe his name was had finally been recovered and brought back to the United States. I felt I had known him but lacked any clarity as to when or how. I could always imagine that his name had been used so much or maybe it was the power of prayer that brought his ordeal to an end, but I felt complete that Christmas eve. I am sure being a hostage is a very difficult situation to be in. Add in years, it is a wonder that some did not try to commit suicide just to end their pain and torment; I am sure some of them had.

Nobody gets left behind unless they chose that for themselves. That saying had to be a motto from something, but it did stick with me. It was the one thing that someone had to believe in no matter how long it would take. None of us were bound by some military code that said we had to do this or that in a certain amount of time. There were those times that we had to pick up the pieces that some other entity had left behind. They never knew and we would never tell them. It was in our honor, so to speak. "Song 91"

My Father was a deeply religious person. Every Sunday, he would reach into the closet, put on his Sunday best, set this black hat with a red feather in its band on his head and off to church he would go with his family in tow.

Every other day was on the art of survival. "Son, the lord helps those who help themselves as long as they can meet in a place once a week and just be as one." I often wondered whether he meant Church, the Lion's Club or the Legion as all three seemed to be on his agenda. That is how I grew up and it stuck with me even after I had lost my memory. Little did I know I was following my own path that I had long ago discovered within the dynamo room; "that place of power."

1992 brought a slight awareness that what I had forgotten was becoming familiar through sight, sound and sometimes a forgotten voice. It had not been an easy transition. My daughter and I were connected at the hip by now with me taking her most everywhere I went. I spent a lot of my days at the Library with her and sometimes without. I finally secured a job at a local Nursing Home as an assistant Nurse's Aide and even had the pleasure of becoming an assistant Girl Scout Leader to fill the void of an absentee Leader. My daughter's class would have been cancelled so I stepped up to the plate and quite unexpectedly put on the Brownie Uniform in my own mind. As they say, "these were the best of times."

My first class in securing a position at the first Nursing Home came with the label, "Whatever it takes." And it took a lot of understanding. I made a good friend of a guy who had been Military as well who joined our class; two men and seven women. I knew his name only as Truscott; he had been with an army unit in Panama during the ouster of Manuel Noriega. As we spent more time together, I realized that his memory and mine were on opposite sides of that endeavor; mine on clean out and his on clean-up. We kept things to ourselves, but on the day we parted; we acknowledged a simple truth to each other. We had been on opposite sides of the equation. He came with the knowledge of Milton, Mass and I left with the other truth of Wilton, NH with none the wiser; even ourselves. The only casualty of our time spent together in the same job was the suicide of one of our classmates. We never saw each other again after that with both of us joining other nursing homes.

The year passed while I kept writing, nursing and saw the many things which came in and out of my dreams always leaving me with that question; "Who am I?" There would always be that morning ritual as I opened my eyes laying there hoping for some miracle that my memory would return all at once. I am glad it did not for I would have missed the important factors.

Each day I awoke, I would ask myself three questions; who am I, where am I and why am I still here? It became almost an obsessive endeavor just before opening my eyes. It was a reminder to honor each waking moment as a time I could not remember what I once forgot; the who, I knew, the where was here and the reason why, I have kept to myself. I never went back to Canada. I look back sometimes smiling to what must have been a real treat for some to see the many letters I wrote back to my family. It was ammunition taken out of my very own words and sent back across the border. They were actions subliminally directed back to me for the most part and to those who were so honestly trying to protect me as I stumbled through trying to learn the truth about myself. My wife had been a classmate of the police chief, while this did not afford me any special treatment or consideration at the time, it did provide for a layer of keeping the Sherriff's Department off my back. I neither knew the reasons why, nor the need to even find out.

It wasn't until I went to a museum in Boston that the first flashes of memory began nudging the back of my mind. I started spending enormous amounts of time at the Boston Public Library yet never taking my thoughts from the Isabella Steward Gardner Art Museum. I researched, I explored and started to understand that all of this was second nature to me as if I had done this sort of thing before; and I had. I did it for survival to preserve what might have been lost but never allowing me to see anything other than what I needed to do; that was to recover my memory fully intact and all that went with it.

Eventually, my interest in the nursing home began to wane about the time that Flight 800 crashed in the Atlantic. The whole concept of having done this before began to take over in my mind and though what seemed a hobby began to stir the memories long embedded in the past.

By this time, random people would be trying to make contact with me as well as few guys from NASA. They never let on that they had an interest, yet they were incapable of understanding what I had experienced as a teenager. In as much as they were observing, I was reading into them. I learned a lot from these guys about myself, my time in Florida and the east coast disaster of the Challenger. It was one of though rare moments that a ghostly image was passed from one of them to me. The transition of a soul from one entity to another is very rare in itself, but I now remember that it was not so strange for me.

I had acquired a soul who had not crossed over to the other side and had given up hope on ever reaching for the stars. Souls have an unusual compulsion to teach the truth of their past and sometimes their future to their host. As for the NASA guys, they could not locate the missing piece that had set them on this study of my behavior. There were truths out there, but I was the wrong guy to be learning them from; I didn't have any association or recollection of aliens whether friendly or hostile. They had a good sense of humor when they learned I was only trying to recover my memory. That would be the last time I would have any respect for the virtual head of NASA. Dan Quail may not have been brilliant, but he was the most honest guy when it came to ethics.

13

Where Eagles Fly

By now, my daughter and I were still spending a lot of time together which now seemed mostly in the Law Library of the Benjamin Crane Public Library in Quincy. I was mesmerized by the amount of Literature and my child's aptitude to sit and read law books. It may not have been the perfect environment for her, but it did allow for a lot of privacy away from pesky observers. It seemed this place had been placed off limits by a higher power with its beautiful mahogany furniture and thousands of books.

Finally, it dawned on me that I had not graduated high school for reasons I alone knew why. Then one day while sitting on the lawn in front of the library, I looked across at Quincy College, down the street to Quincy High School, finally looking over my shoulder. There was a church nestled in next to the Crane Library with its gargoyles firmly attached to its tower. Ugly as they were, their presence, no matter ornate reminded me of the many things which had been left up in the air and needed dealing with as soon as possible. I would go back to school and graduate with a GED but it had to be the perfect place.

I found what I was looking for in Hull, MA which was called Wellspring and provided a secure setting in which to unlock the secrets of my mind. For me, that was an obstacle to be overcome. I was far from stupid, but mathematics seemed to be a stumbling block. It was several weeks into classes that the numbers began to finally make sense and all things became possible. I graduated and was encouraged to take a course on English Literature by a Jesuit Priest at Boston College. He had represented the Adult Education portion of higher education.

My son was already in school while my daughter would be just starting kindergarten. The end of summer found me starting to put my life back together. It was slow to say the least, but Hingham provided a much needed respite from big brother for the most part. Granted, I was still the focus of something I could not quite place my finger on, but in the end, there was no mistaking what any senator would do to keep his seat in government. Had I created more problems for myself by being honest? That answer would be yes and no.

The Clinton Administration came into power on the concept that; "It's the economy stupid." The Bush Administration left power with the notion; "WTF" after a successful campaign removing Iraq from Kuwait. I was left stranded wanting to write, but could not. I had been passed over in the heart of America for reasons that could only be explained that there were already two Franklins and no need for something which did not exist. Graham and Thomas had been propelled whereas I was discarded as a broken toy no longer worthy of political play. I guess my use served well in a devil state better than any state at all, but that was not my honor or duty; mine was to recover me alone. Parting was very mutual.

Then, the First Lady wrote a Book called "It Takes a Village" which left me more confused than understood. I knew what she meant, but it did not sound like her. It wasn't until 1997 that I actually found out that we would finally agree on the content twenty years later in the future. That would be a long time. The theory of time has no relative position as far as I understood it. I did not want to make contact with this First Lady until I was reasonably sure that she was honest yet heartfelt. Those were my experiences from 1997 on even after all the commotions of the Oval Office. It almost felt like Barbara Bush had written it, but the mystery was somewhere half way between.

On a cold January day in 1998, a group of individuals decided to get together to make one last endeavor to wake me from my sleeping state; I am sure no one felt I had lost my memory, it was more the view that I had lost my mind but it was the incessant nagging of that Teaching Soul to learn the truth.

I had decided to do an evening cross country ski in a place called 'The Trustees of Reservations' which was not unusual for me. It was a clear evening, full moon with clean crisp air that felt good while travelling the many paths throughout the area. Little did I know, this would be the opportunity where only those whom I knew in the old days created the perfect meeting place.

Under a full moon in a darkened place, several shadows appeared before me forming a perfect obstacle. As I came to a full stop on my skis, there was the feeling that these were my friends and probably the only ones I truly had because I didn't know them. Out front of the group was a slender woman who spoke in a commanding voice; "It is time we had a chat." Her teeth were perfect in the light of the moon.

I don't know what came over me, but I could not refrain from saying; "Is this going to hurt?" And with that, she unclipped the skis with her poles in a forward motion and moved towards me with her arms outstretched. I didn't know whether to speak or smile as her arms came up around me; the kiss was on both cheeks. She whispered into my ear and spoke very softly. "What have they done to you Mon ami?"

I felt warmth from her touch and softness in her voice. I looked at every face behind her hoping to recognize one of them, but I did not. I was told they represented every nation of the NATO I once knew and with a little humor, a stick of a pin, they learned as I did that most of my memory was gone. The lady said it would not surface without the right criteria. They were satisfied as well as I was that the "nobody left behind rule" still applied no matter how long it took.

With a campfire set, voices of my past filled the night air and Newfoundland Screech was passed amongst the group. I did not partake and had completely given it up just before our little trip into Kuwait in a place called Clinton Harbor.

My wife once told me that on the way back up the Devil's Staircase in Connecticut of August 1990, we stopped at a restaurant. I had a lobster dinner, two bottles of beer, got up from the table and said; "That's it for the drink my dear; this will be the last beer I have until this whole thing is over." I gave no other reason as we headed for Braintree the next morning.

The group was now sitting in a semi-circle around me now. The Lady sat next to me on the snow.

"I have no idea who you are;" I said to her in absolute honesty.

She began speaking to me in French and for some reason; I knew exactly what she was saying. I leaned over placing my hand on her arm and said; "You are the secret." With that, the discussion went to the many things I should have known but had forgotten. A portable light was introduced and passed amongst us while I watched each guy open his jacket and shirt. The light would reflect something only that light would reveal. When it came to my turn, I unzipped my jacket, unbuttoned my shirt and saw nothing over my heart until I flicked on the light.

There was no mistaking what I had seen or disbelieving what the light revealed.

It said; "We came from the water, to it we shall return."

I was flabbergasted but it all began making sense now. They were the ones who had usurped the power from the Royal Canadian Mounted Police. There was nothing more to say as I carefully listened to what had transpired from those days of one dirty business. Instead of getting their man, the RCMP was given a new security service with civilian oversight.

It had been rumored for years that the RCMP and the KGB Foreign Security services had long been in bed together. As this has never been proven beyond a shadow of a doubt, it did remain as a shadow that needed watching. Like all things though, it was just rumor until proven. This evening was about rekindling friendships I could not remember; to which I was quickly brought up to speed on the changes of the last several years. There was no holding back anything. If I could understand the true meaning of Victoria's Secret, it would be tonight that it grew wings.

"I have come from France to ask you a favor which in the old days would not be a request. No one knows I am here and I want to keep it that way."

I nodded my head. There was something about her that reminded me of Ann Eaton which I could not put my finger on, but she was pristine.

"I will help in any way I can;' I said to her.

She smiled and touched my hand with hers. "Did you hear about the TWA Flight to Paris?"

I thought about it for a while and said, "Yes, I was working the 3 to 11 shift at the nursing home when it went down."

"I would like some assistance in finding out what happened to it after leaving New York. There was something on Flight 800 that was never recovered or it may never have been placed onboard."

I knew what she was asking of me. Stuff like this was dangerous and could put my family in jeopardy, especially if it was not an accident. I looked down into the snow where my hand was drawing out a complicated figure of an eagle. Just for that one moment, I allowed my thoughts to go back in time and remember the day I sent a little plastic Eagle that I had removed from a child's juice drink container and sent it to the Embassy of Iraq in Canada. The reason for doing such a thing so close after the end of the first Gulf War really never made sense to me at the time but it was taken as a friendly gesture. Soon after that, Saddam's Gold Reserves were secretly transferred to a Bank in New York somewhere around the World Trade Centers.

I had not known how many people knew that I was from Nova Scotia and a friend, but there were more who knew about me than I had known about them. Secrets were hard to keep when you had no idea who or what the secret was. But this lady sitting next to me, I did not know why but I could not refuse her anything she asked of me.

"Do you know why my dad liked the people of Nova Scotia so much?" She said with this enchanted smile on her face.

I had no idea what to say as I lay back outstretched on the snow moving my legs and arms in a flapping motion on the fresh snow cover. She broke out laughing realizing that I was making a snow angel instead of speaking.

"Something like that;" she said with a smile. My dad loved boats and while sailing the Nova Scotia coastline, he found himself in trouble one day. He was rescued by some fisherman and put up in a house until his boat was repaired. The friendliness of those people stuck in his mind. That is why he always made a point of hiring people from there for his properties. "Does that help explain a few things?"

I thought for a moment as I sat back up before speaking; it did explain a lot, but not everything.

The faces of the men around me began to take on a familiar shade of friendship as they began to stand up and walk towards me. As I stood up, one hand was placed in mine and the other was placed over each of their hearts as they passed by, one by one. The lady who I will now call sincere stood up beside me, reached over and softly kissed my cheek. I felt the sensuality of a spark pass through it and down the spine until it reached my feet. This should have been the moment when I muttered my usual phrase; "feet don't fail me now."

I had no reason to run anywhere for this was my adopted family. As fast as they appeared, they disappeared all in unison as if a bunch of ducklings following their mother down that snow covered path. The guy whom I now worked for had made these paths with his New Holland loader laying down weed fabric and covering it with a stone dust fill. I began to wonder just how much he knew, finally realizing that he knew nothing at all. He had hired and brought me back here for a reason, one that he could never have possibly known. I got my skis back on and decided on making my own path instead of following it any further. It was another hour before I left the wooded area arriving at a flag pole in front of a nursing facility. It was a Beverly Facility and I knew right away where I had parked my car. My time here was coming to an end; I was heading someplace else.

Victoria had filled in the many voids that I hadn't been aware of for a quite a few years and quite frankly, there were more questions instead of answers; I would have to think about this for a while. Then on Valentine's Day, an ad appeared in the Patriot Ledger looking for a handyman to do residential work around Hingham. I answered it and got the job from a charming couple who owned several properties; one in Hingham, another near Otis Air Force Base and the other on the waterfront in downtown Boston. The job lasted until April fool's day of 1999 and in that time, I had been propelled into something I could not fully comprehend.

My first day of work should have given me a clue of what lay before me but I had misread the powers of observation. On the first day I went to work, I could not make it up the hill of the driveway. There was some frozen ice on the ground and I watched helplessly as my mini-van came sliding down backwards almost out into the street with me at the wheel. I couldn't believe it.

I made another attempt, almost making it to the top before I came sliding down again, but this time, I slid off the road into the next door neighbor's back garden. Of course, my old boss came to the rescue pulling my van back onto the roadway with his dump trunk. He just shook his head at me. "What were you thinking?"

"Gees Frank, this is not the place for you without a whole lot of salt & sand next time." Of course, when did I ever take someone else's advice? I backed on down the driveway, out into the street.

It was sanded this time as I drove right up to the top of the hill. I would call it "The Ridge." The next year and a half sent me to the hospital twice, Washington DC twice and to Cape Kennedy once for no reason other than I felt I had to go. Then one day, my employer decided to leave and find another place to live, until a letter surfaced which was left in the owner's home. Actually, he had been my boss of sorts and I believe the letter was addressed to him. It would be years before I actually had a chance to read the letter, but upon seeing it, there was no doubt that it was in my handwriting, almost.

The variations of handwriting are complex for the most part. Someone was quick to inform me of its presence leaving my only option to leave his employment, leave the town and spare my own embarrassment. I was appalled but saw my own handwriting; "feet don't fail me now." Someone wanted me gone from Hingham, forever; I could only imagine who. In the meantime, I was keeping a slight interest in young Kennedy's magazine called "George" and was sad to hear of its low readership and interest. I had my own problems and issues for now.

Victoria had told me that I had been retired with as much unofficial scrutiny as could be tolerated. The only thing that I can say is that when you see the Russian Navy Ensign Flag the next time, its reauthorization and your retirement will coincide in history.

Circumstances had seen to certain things while things would no longer exist. Enjoy what I needed to do, but don't enjoy it too much. She had informed me that I had been under surveillance that September of 1990 when I had visited Portland, Maine before the recovery operation. Her last words were, "don't let them enslave you." Vickie had that kind of sense of humor. In the meantime, I had to get ready for a job that would propel me into pure chaos.

I did not get what she meant, but I assumed there was some hidden meaning she was trying to tell me. How George would play into this, I didn't know.

Portland had a Dry Dock to complete the building of Destroyers. The Scotia Prince Ferry would travel back and forth from Nova Scotia. There was an oil pipeline from there to refineries in Montreal, Canada and last but not least, Fort McKinley was an old military outpost from the Spanish American war era. It was as if this place had been built there just for me. If I had of remembered correctly, I would have known that William McKinley had been assassinated by an Anarchist. Was this another clue from the torch or just another nail in my coffin?

There was something about the Island though that started an era of visions for me. I could see things that hadn't happened yet with so much clarity which left me quite bewildered as to the reason why. Much that I had written the last several years ended up as campfire fuel; I saw to that. I am not sure why, but the things I wrote were beginning to project what I could visualize into the future.

It was not easy and for the first several months, I saw my family only on week-ends. It was difficult but very tolerable. They were safe, but I was not. Here, I was exposed to my past even though I was now isolated from

most outside contact. The ghosts of the USS Eagle, the last
American warship had sunk only a few miles away from
here at the end of the War. Historical aspects were always
in play but I will always beleive

The letter writing campaign to the 1600
Pennsylvania Drive in the early 90's was coming back to
haunt me in strange ways. I saw the missile strike on the
Chinese Embassy, there was the Orion incident over the
China Sea and the Nuclear Submarine Incident with the
Japanese Trawler.

All the while, I had already known that China and
Japan would be the two countries that would provide the
currency to keep our Country functioning in the future;
one above with the other below. The recession that was to
come would be caused by conflicts and we needed not to
have a conflict with our future friends. Besides all of that,
wasn't one of our past Presidents an Ambassador to
China? I did not make the mistake of trying a new letter
writing campaign to The Whitehouse. In the end, I made
things worse.

Finally, on July 16th 1999, young John Kennedy's
plane went down taking his life and that of his wife and
sister-in-law. I was devastated. Very few people had
known that John and I had done some paddle boarding off
Hyannis and had shared some personal issues of missing
our fathers. I knew that I had known him, but our
friendship would remain a secret. Those who knew me,
except my own Brother's in Arms and Victoria of course

suddenly became expendable. There was nothing I could do and what made matters worse was the letter from Hingham that had been left at my old boss's residence. I suppose I lost a good friend because of it while providing a quick means to the end of a divorce.

The letter would inflict many years of shame as it was held up for me to read; there was nothing I could say back then. I do know that whatever brought my employment to an end in Hingham had also brought the young American Prince to his. The reasons may have been different, but the name would always be the same. Had John Kennedy Jr. lived, he would have become the youngest President in the history of the United States; the dime being the key that would deliver its final blow and never leave a trace that would entomb the three of them. I dealt with the pain and decided to move on with my life. I had some experiments to complete.

The nice part of my time at Diamond Cove; I finally understood what happened to Flights 800, 990 & eventually 111. People die, but the water does not once you learn to unlock its secrets. It was a natural gift that I soon learned would become a curse at first then finally a gift. Like the letter that was written, no one I knew had been at fault, none more innocent that me.

14

Striking Back

How do you bring a story to an end? Sometimes, you have to go back to the beginning in order to finish what has been started. Or, you can pick up a poem; I like Ralph Waldo Emerson's Poems for their insight.

"Do not go where the path may lead, go instead where there is no path and leave a trail."

In that moment, the second plane flew into the other building. I could hear the screams on the other end of both lines.

"I have to go now," I said with a calm and reassuring voice switching the phone off. I laid it down on a wrought iron bench beside me. I shouldn't have been so honest with the woman on the phone, but if I worked for someone, honesty had to be part of that package.

The man on the other line was no longer there; that line was dead. I said a prayer for the others as I walked to the center of the garden behind the Gatehouse. I buried the cell-phone beneath the urn. I wasn't hiding it, I had buried it as if that was all I could do; and it was. There was no one to call, even less if I had something to say with no idea why; even if I could; I was caught in a catch 22; I had been enslaved.

It was 2 am when Victoria finally showed up with four men sitting in the garden. I had been in the moment and never heard their arrival. "Note to self, get a dog."

I had been sleeping in the library with the window wide open in a very soft and comfortable chair in the Gatehouse. I smelt the cigar first before it touched my lips and sensed the subtle aroma of an individually rolled Havana Cigar. My hand went up in a split second grasping the person's wrist before it could actually touch my lips. The smell of Coco Chanel danced across my senses as I relaxed my grip on her wrist.

"Hi Vic", I paused; "you know there was nothing I could do about today." There was only silence at first with the heavy breathing of her being caught off guard as well.

"I know. We just came from Hingham. You are in danger." I already knew that.

I flicked on the lamp over my right shoulder and looked at a very tired face with lines on the skin that were now showing her age. There were crow's feet at the edge of each eye and I realized that her concern was for me.

"Come outside, the house is bugged;" she said without batting an eye. It was the way of the world now.

I almost forgot protocol and blurted out "What?" But the instinct does take over as I slowly pushed myself to my feet. I exited the Library past the New York cutting board that the owner had purchased a year earlier. I eventually made my way out into the garden through the screened porch. Before me stood four men all standing at attention, but it wasn't with distaste. I couldn't refrain from making a snide comment.

"You guys loaded for bear, or what?" With that said, smiles broke across their faces and the hardware hanging from their shoulders was pointing down. No, these guys would not be going to California; they would follow Victoria right back to World's End or from wherever she had come from. World's End was a piece of land in Hingham that was managed by something she had held very dear over the years.

In unison, it was the middle finger that came up which left no doubt as to how they really felt. They were a little older yet still faithful to her Word; she was the 5th Republic in its essence. For Victoria, if and when she was called; she would take the 5th each and every time.

The Legion has a motto that the special ones only know about; it is "faithful until death." The look is unmistakable. It was on their faces, but more so in their eyes; Victoria had that power over them.

"Someone has to get to 'the powers to be' before they make a mistake," she said without batting an eye.

Everyone lowered their heads to the ground and not a sound was made until I broke the silence.

"I will do it," I said, "But I want to do it my way; I need a few days to research some poetry. "The message has to target one person and one person alone so only they will understand."

Vickie placed her hands on her hips and said for all to hear; "brilliant, absolutely brilliant; they won't be expecting it." And with that, the garden became empty except for the sounds coming from the graveyard directly behind the gatehouse. I agreed with what she said, but hey, there had to be an easier way than sacrificing my own security. There was just a whisper of sound and a flash of lights departing from over my head. I could feel the warm blast of air coming from France's newest creation in whisper mode. In the meantime, I had a job to do.

It took me a couple of days to put the package together. Poetry is an art form but I couldn't tell her what I was going to do any more than I could convince myself that it would work anyway. All eyes were on Afghanistan; the Buddhists wanted the desecration of Buddhist's sand and stone structures stopped, the Evangelists wanted the hostage taking of Missionaries by the Taliban stopped, the Pakistani's wanted more military hardware with the soft shells of Ben Franklins' in their coffers and finally there were those who could see the importance of future Flanders fields where poppies could grow without regulation. Then there was the United States Air Force who wanted to avenge the tribulations that had been inflicted at the Khobar Towers in Saudi Arabia. According to the tally sheets that were still being kept, the Air Force had missed the advance warnings, the subliminal tit for tat of too many shadows trying to keep the US engaged. Add up all those scenarios while trying to convince a President who felt so frustrated that he wasn't being taken seriously, was a feat that could not possibly be accomplished; but I would try.

On Friday morning, I launched a blue kayak from the shores of Diamond Cove with no concept how I would get this thing delivered, someone to take me seriously, trickle down the amount of Oil Tankers entering and exiting the Harbor and give the Coast Guard a needed boost of up to date hardware and boats. The fact that I didn't want to be sacrificed in the interim was playing heavy on my mind as I paddled over to the Canadian Oil Terminal. Only one tanker was hooked up to the number 2 Pipeline which would play in my favor.

I paddled up into the Fore River area just passing a 31 foot Coast Guard Cutter on my portside. I was no threat to them, but in the back of my mind, I couldn't help trying to rationalize that a phone call might be better than this; but who would take me seriously?

I passed under the Fore River Bridge which joins Portland to South Portland. I had a good look of how many oil tankers were up river off-loading; there was only one at the Irving Terminal. I made my turn in a Carolina kayak realizing what I needed to do as I passed under the bridge once again. I stopped for a brief moment to honor the guy whose line had gone dead just a few days earlier. It was now or never. I could have warned him that morning, but he had a destiny with a young Prince who would ask him that which had left a Y on my left shoulder. I had to remain neutral as my responsibility was to the truth and the truth alone.

It took me fifteen minutes to arrive at the outer dock of the Coast Guard Station where I reached down by my side into the kayak and threw the zip-locked bag up on the dock filled with nothing but papers. There was a Petty Officer braiding lines on the dock as I said to him; "Give this to your Commanding Officer for the First Lady."

Hey, she was a librarian at one time in her life, so where better to send these papers?

Actually, there were those who were silently up to speed on what the First Lady actually was, but rest assured, none of them had been expecting this. The First lady was the Saint Laurent, a Canadian destroyer with the number 205. Unfortunately, no one could figure out that 205 was the room that held the FBI offices in Portsmouth from where this whole charade had begun. The Petty Officer blew a circuit in all rationales of emotions and proceeded to arrest me. It was then that I figured out that the FBI and the Coast Guard were so far apart on Intelligence matters. I made my debut onboard the buoy tender, "Shackleton." It was not funny. I'd like to say that the greater part of damage that was done to my knees happened with handcuffs on being held down on my knees on a cold iron deck, but I won't. Everyone had a job to do, but unfortunately, my knees became collateral damage. I would live.

There are a lot of stupid things I have done in my life, but this would not be one of them if thousands of people could have been saved from the bad intelligence that was being manifested for reasons I did not know at the time. I was beginning to feel like the First Lady when she slipped her tow and sank just off the North Carolina coast.

It took sometime before I was finally wrestled into an area on coast guard property that would provide for a quiet interview and some self-evaluation. The first person to show up was the local Federal Agent who assumed I needed privacy more than a show of media.

"Is there anything you would like to share at this time?" He was a short stout gentleman who I would trust to have my back in any given situation, but this was not one of them. I knew he would be contacting the Secret Service fellow at the Bush compound pretty shortly.

Within the hour, a gentleman arrived wearing a Secret Service blue pull-over with its name emblazoned front and back. If it was meant to impress, I failed to see the logic in it considering what he would finally read in the zip-lock bag.

My handcuffs were removed upon his request and I was escorted into the coast guard compound to be interviewed and photographed. I was humbled by my situation, but by now, I realized that there would be many Americans humbled by the death of thousands of individuals who would be fighting for something they could not possibly understand and would not after this day; I had to try.

I told him all leaving out nothing; I worked for a compassionate individual who truly believed in patriotism whatever the cost. I told him about my work on the island just across the harbor. I had my picture taken and then was told to never return here again which I then nodded my head and said, "You can count on that!"

My kayak was lowered back into the water while I was being escorted back out to the covered area of the docks. I managed to get back into the kayak with two coast guardsmen holding each end to stabilize it. I had almost made it away when the Agent's cell phone rang. He motioned to the men still attending me to make sure I didn't leave the dock until he returned.

My heart sank as I now realized that George had viewed everything in the bag and the message had hit home. The Secret Service agent returned with a look on his face of "arrest him" that now had my attention. I stretched out my leg until it came to rest on the foot stop deep within the kayak which kept a paddler from slipping into its hull. I pressed my foot twice down until it clicked. The

Agent was watching my every move; I never took my eyes off his.

I raised my hand from inside the kayak and slipped it over the side into the water where he and I both knew, there was a mystery in the making.

"Stop, leave him be" and with a look of sheer unknowing, he asked that one question; "Who gave you this information?"

There was nothing I could say but I said it anyway. "The Ocean, it does not lie." Our eyes held each other's focus and without any cue from me, he said; "you know we lost one of our people on the 11th floor the other day."

"I know, I read it in the paper. I can sympathize with such a loss as tragic as that." The silence was so loud with both Coast Guard guys now looking at each other.

"You can go and relay to him that this is not acceptable." I nodded my head, but I did not tell him that he was her; I would keep this knowledge to myself for years to come.

I paddled from the Coast Guard Station across the stern of the oil tanker named "Bethel Straus" where a crewman was standing on the upper bridge. I caught the one finger salute as a tribute, not an insult. I clicked the foot-pedal one more time within the kayak to send the signal for the DOLPHIN to stand down. She had been preprogrammed into position to assist if my freedom had not been reacquired from the Coast Guard Station. I had been taught to paddle softly but always to carry a big stick.

I managed to make it to Diamond Cove without incident where my employer was now waiting with this ghastly look on her face. The Coast Guard had called her looking for any information on my emotional status; there was none that she could share. I wasn't embarrassed so much that I didn't feel the sorrow that I had failed in achieving a future peace.

Congress was at logger heads, both political parties had dug in before this thing and the only solution that would come out of my sacrifice was the fact that war was a foregone conclusion. It didn't matter where, who or why. People were going to die and keep on dying until everything had been exhausted.

I pulled the kayak up on the shoreline and waited for what was coming. My boss was sitting on the shoreline.

"What were you thinking? You know the Coast Guard called me asking about you and told me what you did."

I removed my life vest without a word sitting down on the tip of the kayak.

"I have just had a very bad day so please don't badger me; there is nothing to say." That was Friday afternoon. The following Monday, the Portland Herald broke the news of what had happened on the local page. It wasn't funny, but miraculously, what I had set out to do; would be accomplished in other ways.

In the days that followed, the President of the United States showed up to speak with the Coast Guard. Funding was granted for new vessels & equipment while harbor traffic was slowed down to a trickle. Not bad even though I probably ruined my life. I had made a very difficult choice that Friday, but I was still alive to remember it, not so much as The Thinker, but in retrospect; The Thinker had finally stepped out from the deep.

I sat in the garden the morning the air force bombed the hell out of Afghanistan and just smiled. I felt I had watched the image of Moby Dick take us all under. The truth was my past; it was my present and would be my future; I needed to go to the place where nobody knew I had existed.

The Chinese have a saying about the good and bad in life; they call it the Ying and the yang. I would learn when the time was right that all I needed to do was drop the why and all the bad would just appear; making sense of it all. There is no mistaking the power within a truth.

Note to self; "Get a dog without a ball that had a President's image on it; the Secret Service will not be impressed."

In the years that followed, it felt like I carried the weight of the world on my shoulders. I had lived most of my life touching base with myself; sometimes in the past to see where I had been. Sometimes, I would look in the mirror and realize that the most precious gift was here in the now. Finally, the phasing into the future would leave me with that one infinite understanding. This should have been something that I would take to my grave, but I didn't.

My faith was unshakeable, my future unmistakable and my hope; yes, my hope. I would have to consider if hope was even acceptable under these circumstances. Then I remembered my father's grave stone. At the bottom was inscribed these words; "Hiding in Thee." Each one of us could find meaning in these three words, but none as vivid as the smile which finally broke across my face. Like the little flower in the field or the Flower Class corvette in Halifax harbor which was to have been my retirement; my only destiny was to survive. Sitting on a rock has no meaning without hope, but it does provide a place in which to ponder the past, the present and my future. As for the chest that my father had once showed me; it would remain a mystery until such time the correct criteria would waken it from its sleep.

Two months later as I was leaving Logan Airport for what I thought was my last time to Paris, France; I could not help but think about Remembrance Day. There were soldiers with weapons maintaining vigilance in and outside of the airport now. The United States had picked up from where the Soviets had left off with the new battle plan on Iraq. I could hear my thoughts telling me not to get involved with that Iraq thing, but rest assured, I would be falling into that manifested trap as well. But for now, it was time to rest and let my mind come to a rest if only for a few days.

I would be once again in the City of Light paying my respects to all concerned. Five days in Paris can change anyone's plans; it sure did mine. The old Mayor was now the President, the Unknown was about to become known and last but not least; I would be returning to a completely different country back in the United States mired in paranoia with imaginary enemies at every door.

I remembered back to a day when a conference had been given on friendship & security in Pugwash. I had been standing on a wooden crate outside of an open window on the side of the old lobster canning factory. It now served as the meal hall and conference center. I might have been seven years old at the time.

The exercise was on how to enter a room as a peace participant with others already in place ready to negotiate a peace and or agreement. The first person to enter the room was this elderly man. He was introduced by the administrator and asked to take his place at the table. The subject was on trusting other nations represented by individuals to be frank & honest.

It was a horrible failure from start to finish until this woman in a black & white outfit stood up and explained why none of this was working. She was what I would call an observer who quite clearly set the framework for the rest of the conference. This gal pointed out that if you enter a room with hate on your mind, it will not disappear in 2 hours or in 2 weeks. If you enter a room with distrust on your mind, it will not disappear; more than likely ending up with no trust at all. But, if you enter a room with an open mind, believing that everyone else in the room has an open mind; then anything can be achieved.

She walked up to the podium as graceful as anyone could be in that given moment. She turned with both hands clasped together positioned beneath her chin.

"Gentlemen, your Nations have done you an injustice by sending you here. Your hopes are burdened by your fears. How can you trust the next person to you if you can't trust yourself? This is not a poker game or something you have to win in order to take back to your governments. You left your humanity at the door before you entered and brought in your insecurity as your motivation to be here."

"My recommendation is for all of you to return home or take the remainder of the day and meet one on one. There are comfortable chairs all around the property with inspiring views of the environment. Be yourselves and think what you would like to leave as a legacy for your own families. It is not about conquering at this conference; it is about preserving humanity for the generations that we pray will be following you."

The look on every one of those men's faces was either distaste or humility. I felt like I was the only one who understood where this woman was coming from and I probably was. I watched as the men got up from their chairs and sauntered out into the sunlight where they dispersed into their own little groups.

I stayed at the window to overhear the administrator chatting with the Nun.

"Weren't you a little hard these participants?" said the Administrator of the Conference.

"Not at all," she said with a smile on her face. "There was only one man in the group I was talking to and that was the bully with the blinders on. Someone had done their work quite cleverly before this Conference had begun."

The man holding the stack of papers in his arms just shook his head and said; "I don't know how you do this in reading through the harsh exteriors of people, but it has to be a Godsend for you."

She looked up at the rafters clutching the thing hanging from a chain around her neck and said as if only for the cobwebs to hear; that could be seen from my position. "The Lord works in mysterious ways."

I was so intent on trying to look up at the ceiling from my window position, I did not realize that the wood was wet beneath my feet in time as the wooden crate rolled out from beneath me. My chin came to rest on the window sill with my feet now firmly planted on the ground.

Across the room, the woman looked over at me while saying to the Administrator; "Only through a child's eyes can we ever hope to see the truth."

Her smile was intoxicating, her voice inspiring and her thoughts; let me just repeat what she had just said.

"The Lord does work in mysterious ways."

The call for pre-boarding of Air France to Boston nudged me out of my dream. With only a Canadian Passport in my hand, I boarded with a smile upon my face. There were a few nods from the sidelines from new friends who would remain behind as if I had never arrived in the first place. The flight was long yet entertaining to say the least and upon arrival at Logan, the INS did not hesitate in wanting to send me back to Paris on the next flight. I did not have the necessary papers according to the female Immigration Inspector.

It would be another fifteen minutes of waiting for me until a Supervisor called the Inspector into a room to discuss my dilemma. In a few minutes as the door closed behind her as she was leaving the enclosed office, all I could hear was her saying; "he's back!" as she made her way

to the counter between us.

I took no insult from her remark and smiled as if I knew absolutely nothing. New York had announced my impending arrival but it had been overlooked at Logan International. It took a few extra minutes before I was released to recover my baggage and be on our way. I had left an impression in Paris, an expression in Houston and a whole lot of egg on Washington's face, but there was no harm done.

The media leak a couple of months ago from the local page of the Portland Press Herald was still causing me a bit of embarrassment, but in the end, I realized that the Lord does work in mysterious ways. I smiled one last time as I passed a Massachusetts State Trooper at the exit beyond Customs. I could hear his faint whisper behind me; "Welcome home, Franklin."

I stopped without turning and said; "thank-you." I looked down at my chest and imagined a pair of dolphins emblazoned on my coat over my heart. It was time to go to work.

The Deep Ocean Logging Platform with Hydrographic Instrumentation and Navigation (DOLPHIN)

www.ingramcontent.com/pod-product-compliance
Lightning Source LLC
Chambersburg PA
CBHW070446260626
47161CB00004B/1216